I0617680

THE AGENCY
Volume Five

Heart Shot

Knight Takes Queen

ELIZABETH
LAPTHORNE

The Agency Volume Five
ISBN # 978-1-78430-541-3
©Copyright Elizabeth Lapthorne 2015
Cover Art by Posh Gosh ©Copyright 2015
Interior text design by Claire Siemaszkiewicz
Totally Bound Publishing

Published in 2015 by Totally Bound Publishing, Newland House, The Point, Weaver Road, Lincoln, LN6 3QN, United Kingdom.

Totally Bound Publishing is a subsidiary of Totally Entwined Group Limited.

HEART SHOT

Prologue

Emily

Emily Camber puffed heavily as she ran for her life. She pounded the soles of her sneakers on the hard ground and focused her brown eyes with laser-like precision ahead of her. Sweat beaded and ran down her face, also trickling down the indentation of her spine. Her ponytail swished in time to the movement of her body. Strands of hair grazed her neck and shoulders — but nothing could distract her.

Focusing intently on placing one foot in front of the other as fast as she could manage, she ignored everything except her actions. She couldn't falter now. Emily disregarded the burning in her calves, the fiery contraction of fatigued muscles. She rasped, struggling for breath as she continued through the pain.

Everything had narrowed to outrunning her demons.

To escape.

To freedom.

Doubts, questions and fear mingled with the pain.

What the hell am I doing? Or more importantly – what am I going to do now?

Emily glanced at the treadmill's readout. She slowed the pace from a flat out run to a fast jog. Her usual half hour of running had finished more than ten minutes ago, which explained her physical exhaustion. She needed to cool down slowly, or her muscles would cramp later on.

Catching her breath at the far easier pace, she chewed over the thoughts she'd come to the gym to try to sort out. Her dissatisfaction with her work had been steadily growing over the last six months. At first she'd simply thought she was in a funk – overworked and starting to feel the effects of the stress inherent in her line of business.

Emily had taken a well-earned week to relax along the coast down at Brighton. She'd read a book and taken numerous walks along the pebbled shoreline. Mostly, she'd just enjoyed the feel of wind on her cheeks and the light scent of salt in the air.

The first time she'd felt the cool snap of the breeze blowing around her she'd automatically started to calculate the effect upon the trajectory of her bullet. It was second nature for her to work out the factor of resistance it would have on the speed...then she realized this time there was no target. She had no sniper's hideout or any need to sit still and patient for hours while she waited for the perfect moment.

This time there would be no death on her hands.

As a small child she'd been afraid of the monsters that lurked in the dark. Emily had experienced more than her fair share of nightmares where she'd been chased by tall, shadowed demons she couldn't outrun no matter how she struggled. Her mother and father had comforted her that such things didn't exist. Now she knew better, but not the way most adults did. There were no shades of gray, no hesitation on what kinds of monster did or didn't exist.

She *knew* there were monsters out there. Dangerous, horrible people who did unspeakable things for no reason other than they could. Emily had learned years ago that there was only one thing you could do to people like that.

Kill them.

And that, she discovered, created another style of monster — those who could kill and continue onward with blood on their hands. People like her, who could live with the knowledge of having taken lives for no reason other than *they* could. They were different to the monsters they'd slain — but that didn't make them any less tarnished.

Emily slowed the treadmill once again, now walking at a quick clip. The sweat cooled on her body. Even as she shivered she wondered if it was her thoughts or the chill that caused her to do so. At first, she'd been certain her skills with almost any gun available could be used for good. She had this talent, why not use it to help rid the world of just a few of the bad guys?

But this sideline had proven far more lucrative than her non-existent journalism career. Rent, utility and all her other bills had pressured her into accepting that for now — only a short time, she'd assured herself — but she'd take on more and more contracts.

Five years later and Emily had to be honest, she hadn't written a thing in months and it had been almost a year since anyone had bought a piece from her. She needed to take stock of her life, decide if this 'sideline' was really the path she wanted to follow.

And there lay her conundrum. While she could write passably well, her only marketable skill was her uncanny accuracy with all forms of weaponry. She could shoot the bull's-eye on a target nine times out of ten tries at over five hundred meters. Her statistics only got better as that distance closed. If she were brutally truthful, Emily didn't see the problem with working for her government—in the most roundabout and completely deniable of ways—and ridding the world of monsters.

She had her own code. Under no circumstances would she touch children, and she demanded to be given enough time on every contract to research the target herself. If she wasn't convinced the person needed to die, she'd refuse the contract and return the money. Emily didn't doubt that she performed a good and sometimes necessary evil. She could feel the tension, the stain of so much death begin to take a toll on her soul.

A vibration at her waist made her jerk and almost fell from the treadmill. In a swift motion she pulled the beeper from her workout pants and read the small screen.

999-James

"Well, shit." She pressed a button and replaced the beeper. Climbing off the treadmill she then stretched.

The man who called himself James was her contact through the backchannels in the government. Emily had met the man once, at the graduation ceremony where she'd studied Literature at University. He'd pointed out that word of her talent had come to his division's notice and they wanted to use her skills once in a while.

Emily was fairly certain James was not the man's real name. What he'd told her had been true enough according to his body language, so maybe it was a family name, or one of his middle names. Much like the man itself, it was a lie wrapped in truth, which summarized their entire working relationship.

Even the covert branches of any respectable service couldn't be seen killing terrorists or murdering men and women who continued to slip through the cracks of the justice system. While the public never mourned the death of the truly depraved, and the media continued to cry for harsher punishments and a greater moral accounting, the wheels of change turned slowly and red tape still stifled even the most underhand of services.

Murder had many costs attached to it.

And that was where James wanted her, and presumably a small number of others, to come in. Emily was completely deniable. She'd been carefully told on that first day that she wasn't on any books, there were no personnel files on her, no tax forms, no expenditure claims. Except for the fact that James contacted her with the details and timeline he required, she had zero contact with anyone, anywhere.

After a text confirming completion and photo from her untraceable mobile phone, money would magically appear in her account twenty-four hours later.

Collecting her key and small hand towel, Emily then climbed off the treadmill. She dabbed at her face and neck. Back at her locker, she unlocked the door. She pulled out her bag and decided to skip the shower she'd planned on taking. After gathering her belongings she left the gym.

Turning in the opposite direction to where her car was parked, Emily slipped on a pair of sunglasses. The dark lenses were a perfect cover for her actions. She checked the windows she walked past for any sign of a tail.

Emily crossed the street, turned right then immediately left. She glided past the busy shops and monitored any people she recognized as being repetitious. After doubling back and walking a complex pattern full of many turns, she was satisfied no one was following her. Unzipping her bag she then felt past her purse and the assorted junk that accumulates in anyone's gym pack until she found her two phones. Her personal mobile was an android, the other a small, cheap disposable with a tiny, four megapixel camera.

It was this latter phone she pulled out. Relative to what one could buy on the market nowadays it was ancient, but it served her purposes. Prepaid and completely clean it was serviceable and could be discarded as soon as she was finished with it. The camera might've been decrepit, but it took pictures clearly and she could send the proof required to James without being traced.

James was the only person who had this number, and the only one who was in the contacts list. Checking around her again, she then called him.

"I thought we agreed I could take a few months off," she said the moment he answered. "It's been three weeks, and I haven't made any decisions yet. What's going on?"

"Em, you know how special you are," James' tone was clearly cajoling. Emily scanned the street and continued to walk, not swayed by his honeyed tone. "This is a special circumstance. There's no one quite like you. You know I wouldn't have called if this wasn't serious."

"I'm not special," she insisted bluntly. "I just make your life easier, James. I can do what few others associated with you can. Let's cut the crap."

"Of course you're special, darling," James' tone deepened, warmed. Emily thought she could detect a faint hint of a Caribbean accent, but she couldn't be sure. Like everything else related to James, it was a mystery, and impossible to guess what was real, what was a lie, and whatever lay in between.

Paranoia and suspicion were tools of the trade when one was an assassin, she'd discovered.

"That's bullshit," Emily said, then sighed. "You have tons of people working for you—a veritable army, figuratively speaking. You have more power and influence at your fingertips that I know of in any other man. It shouldn't be a problem for you to give me time."

"It's true I have many favors owed me, and a lot of influence, as you say," James replied. "But time is one of those slippery things I have no control over. I need the full package and you're the best. I'm calling now because I know you'll want a few days to conduct surveillance and assure yourself it's all right. Besides, you'll need it. He's government connected and will have bodyguards up the arse. This is a harder case and why I need you."

Emily frowned as she paused at a flower stall. Slinging her bag high over her shoulder, she kept a hand free as she bent to smell a bunch of cornflowers. She used the movement to covertly check her tail again. Outwardly appearing focused on the stall, she moved to a tub of pink roses. That let her glance the other way up the street without being blatant about it.

"Em?"

"The challenge of working with you never gets old," she hedged. "But I'd decided to regroup, maybe even try my hand at something else. I don't want to get sucked back in again. I'm serious when I say I'm thinking about getting out of the business."

"Em, you're a natural. I've never known anyone better. I know we keep our distance, for both our sakes, but I've kept tabs on you. On your work. You won't be able to do anything else. Trust me."

Pursing her lips together, she frowned darkly. Emily felt the truth of that statement deep in her soul. She was stubborn however, and determined to do these things on her own terms, under her own conditions. No one could bully her, or force her to pull that trigger. In her heart, in the most secret places of her mind, she worried that James spoke the truth. That this was her purpose, her overwhelming skill — murdering people.

Not something a girl could be proud of, really.

Running from her nature was not smart, it would be better to accept it. Emily insisted to herself that while it might be her calling, she could control the circumstances, the contracts she took and those she slayed. No one, not James, not the government, and certainly not her non-existent partner or lover, could take that from her.

"Give me the details. I'll look into it and text you in two to three days with whether I accept your terms or not."

"Fantastic, I knew I could count on you," James spoke quickly, as if afraid if he took too long she'd change her mind. "I'm texting through his photo and details right now. The target is Keyton Marshall and he's a mid-level analyst for one of the government branches. He's been selling sensitive data from a clandestine division to anyone with deep enough pockets…"

Equal parts resigned and curious, Emily dug her free hand into her bag. In seconds she pulled out the pen and notebook she always carried with her. Originally she'd convinced herself it would be in case she came across something she could write an article about, but years ago she'd realized the majority of the time she used it to jot down notes and thoughts for missions like this.

Despite her weariness, the familiar spark of a new hunt, a fresh case, zinged through her body. She couldn't lie to herself. She loved this part of her work. All too quickly she knew she would uncover secret dealings, corruption, degradation and often unspeakable acts of pure evil. But as she made encrypted notes to herself, Emily hoped this case would give her back some of her former invigoration.

* * * *

Finlay

Finlay Mann entered his boss's office with curiosity.

"Shut the door, Fin," Preston Jones said without lifting his head from the report he was scanning. Fin paused, perplexed. Mentally he ran through the last few days. He couldn't find anything major that he'd fucked up, so he relaxed and pushed the door closed.

"Troy's surgeon called a few minutes ago. He'll be stuck in the hospital for at least a few more days, possibly a week depending on how quickly he recovers," Preston explained as Fin took a seat.

Fin tensed. He took a second to collect himself before he spoke. Preston Jones was a good boss, but he was still a manager to Fin's mind. There was a certain protocol when it came to them that both he and his sometime partner, Troy, adhered to.

Only admit to what you have to.

Shaking his long blond hair from his eyes, Fin then sat taller in his chair. He kept his gaze alert as he stared at Preston, looking for any signs or indication of an undercurrent to his words.

Preston was tall, large and dark-skinned. He'd retained the fit physique of a man of action. Despite having been a team leader and desk-bound for the last five years, Preston had a solid reputation and hadn't seemed to forget the often volatile and spur-of-the-moment nature of field work.

Fin respected the man. Even though he knew where his agents were coming from, Preston wasn't a soft touch. He could chew a man out with only a steely glance, and had been known to make fresh recruits, not cut out for this work, cry like babies.

Fin hoped he wasn't about to be on the receiving end of another stern lecture.

"He was only grazed on the shoulder," Fin said with deceptive calm. His stomach knotted, for Troy could have been hurt far worse. Troy was not a member of the Agency—not officially. Fin hadn't been able to settle with any partner over the space of two years, no one really understood or fit with him. So when he'd met a Consultant on one mission, and they'd worked well together, Fin had convinced Preston to let them continue to collaborate when Fin needed someone to watch his back.

Fin feared very little in this world—but having to break in a new partner was definitely top on his list.

"I believe there was also the mild matter of a punctured lung and three cracked ribs," Preston replied with a small smile. He looked up for the first time. Fin's stomach unclenched.

If this was another ass-reaming there wouldn't be the smile, or the humor in his boss's tone.

"Pfft." Fin waved a hand in casual dismissal. "You wait. Give it a few more days for Troy to find his feet and he'll be driving everyone in the entire hospital mad. We'll be lucky if the staff don't riot. He's fine."

"Yes, neither of you gentlemen deal well with boredom. I'll give you that," Preston mused. "Whether your friend will be out of commission for a week or six, which means you'll be on solitary duties for at least the near future. And that brings me to why I called you in. I know it's not your usual thing, but I'm going to assign you to bodyguard duties for a short time."

Fin was shocked. Frozen, he merely blinked as his brain tried to assimilate the words.

"Bodyguard duties?" he repeated, feeling stupid. Preston's comment seemed insane, almost as if it were a joke. Fin remained silent, expecting the man to crack a smile and admit he'd been hooked. But that didn't occur.

"Yes," Preston replied.

The man offered nothing more, and Fin swallowed hard. Fin didn't miss the way Preston eyed him up and down before meeting his gaze again.

"I'm not certain your wardrobe even contains the quiet, sober suits necessary," Preston finally added. "But you've surprised me before with the various ensembles I've witnessed. And you've never let the Agency down, so I have confidence you can rise to this challenge."

Fin's outfits were the stuff of many office jokes and inter-agency legend. Brightly colored, sometimes even outlandishly patterned, Fin loved wearing all manner of blazers, scarves and slacks. With his long hair, snazzy outfits and casual manner he often was mistaken initially for what he honestly could have become—a fabulously wealthy playboy, one of the many rich fancies who had nothing to do all day but be idle and get into mischief.

Word of his enormous trust fund had taken mere minutes to circulate around the Agency when he'd started. Spies could be the worst kind of gossips when it came to personal information.

Initially, most had assumed he'd only been dabbling in espionage to while away the time until the interest rates on his capitol grew. Fin had proved them all wrong, and spectacularly so. With his connections and air of languid ease, Fin could usually talk his way into anywhere from the snottiest gallery affair to the haughtiest debutante's ball.

His connections, prestige and knowledge of how people from all walks of life ticked had proven invaluable. Fin privately thought his work was the best high he'd ever experienced, clean or not.

"But Preston...really? *Bodyguard* duties? Is this because the powers that be are pissed about a civilian getting shot? Because as I explained to them—"

"It's nothing of the sort," Preston assured him. "I just don't want you chatting up half the office staff or hanging around here, lolling about and giving us a bad name."

Fin grinned. He could read between the lines. Preston didn't want him flirting with the ladies in the office or getting caught with his hand up someone's skirt.

He loved everything there was about women, from the way they'd flush, the sparkle they all got in their eyes to the millions of variations the form of a luscious woman could contain.

Each one was different, and he adored them all.

"You're just worried that with a whole week of my being here I'll snare a bunch of hearts and they'll be distraught when I head back out into the field," Fin teased.

Preston shook his head. "I prefer you being under heavy fire in a burning warehouse. That charming grin and those innocent blue eyes don't work against bullets. They force you to use that very smart brain you're blessed with. It's no effort at all for you to smile sweetly at the girls and coax them into the stairwell for a few kisses. You've been doing that all your life. I'd prefer to keep you sharp."

On one of his first cases Fin had been pinned down in a burning factory, under heavy gunfire. Troy had been following his own leads and they'd found themselves trapped. Backed into working together they quickly hatched a plan. Taking turns to lay suppressing fire around them, they'd worked in tandem and saved what they could from the mission. They'd both escaped with hardly a scratch.

It had been the first time many in the Agency had seen anything other than an idle playboy dabbling at cloak and dagger games from Fin. Preston and many of the other managers had seen some of the depth he held, and his reputation had grown because of it.

"I can't imagine you want me to guard someone where the situation is going to end in a right royal cock-up. My forte doesn't run to over-analyzing the moves of everyone in the room. I don't have the patience for that."

"Oh no," Preston assured him. "This is strictly information gathering. I just want you to shadow Keyton Marshall for the week. He's got the ear of the Prime Minister, and you should know he's the main go-between for this Agency and the PM. The last thing we need is to make a fuss. Marshall always has three or four lackeys around him, like his personal assistant and fresh-faced, aspiring politicians and whatnot. You're not there to look menacing or like a bodyguard at all. I want you to gather information, inform Marshall his safety is guaranteed and blend in... Well, as much as *you* can at least."

Fin frowned further. He'd never aspired toward politics—his father would have been all for that. Neither did Fin usually get along well with that set. He found them largely to be a smarmy lot. All sweetness to your face, just waiting for your back to be turned or a decent opportunity to present itself. Then it was every man for himself and those not malicious enough to stab the other in the back usually fell far and fast.

"You know that's not my scene..." Fin sighed as Preston merely raised an eyebrow.

"I thought you could fit in anywhere? Talk to anyone?" Preston said with deceptive mildness.

"Well, I didn't say I couldn't do the job. Just that it wasn't my scene," he protested. "Do you have any idea how deadly dull this will be? That lot consider backstabbing a delightful pastime. Not to mention all the kissing arse and backroom games they indulge in."

"I'm not asking you to get us more funding, or assist in cutting some of the red tape—though I'd not turn down any help you managed to get us either. You're there to monitor Marshall and see if you can find out whether he's been turned, or is willingly selling information. This isn't a party invitation, but a proper mission, Mann. Understood?"

Fin nodded, resigned himself to a week of boredom, social prattle and walking a pace behind his target. Meek, mild and unnoticeable wasn't usually within his job parameters, but he could do his best. He tried to look on it as a challenge, and wondered how many of the political men he would wind up in his stay there.

"I don't suppose you would get a proper haircut?" Preston added. The wry twist to his mouth showed he was only being half serious.

"Pierre insists this cut makes me look like a prince," Fin grinned. "Okay, so I'm not really there to bodyguard, though that's evidently what we're telling Marshall. So what am I *really* supposed to be doing?"

"There's something going on in his circle of cronies." Preston handed over a file from his desk. "I've got nothing but instinct here, that's why you're going in supposedly to guard him. There isn't anything in Marshall's phone records, expenses, his financials are all above board and add up. It's been driving me insane. I can't find a shred of evidence, but I'm positive someone thinks he's doing something and speaking quietly in all the right ears to that effect. There's a person or group of people out there who want to cause a world of trouble for Marshall, and they're doing a very good, albeit subtle, job of it. Reputation is everything over there. Even if Marshall is as clean as the Virgin Mary if too many people start listening to the whispers he'll be shut out faster than you can sneeze."

"He's the only reliable link we have to the PM?"

"Yes, he's the only one who's stood by the Agency through thick and thin."

"Okay then. What am I looking out for?"

"You're recon only. I want you to make a note of who he talks to, who he's checking into, who he gets in contact with — everything. Even who he is supposed to be talking to and doesn't. Like I said there is nothing concrete, only my instinct."

"And enough of a whiff to have me follow this schmuck around for a week," Fin added. "So, you must either be desperate to get me out of the office, or fairly certain something's off."

"It's both," Preston replied with a serious tone.

Fin chuckled.

"I'm supposed to go unnoticed for a whole week? Well, I'm sure I can rise to the challenge. Just be warned, I'll bring out my most obnoxious outfits upon my return."

"And you will have to wear your piece," Preston insisted.

Fin made a sour face.

"You serious? Aw, get off it. You know I hate carrying."

"You won't have anyone there to watch your back, and what kind of legitimate bodyguard doesn't carry a gun?"

Fin made another face, but had to nod in resignation. Martial arts weren't his forte, and no one who took a glance at him would believe he could intimidate anyone with the size of his body alone.

He hated carrying a gun. Not just because they ruined the look and fall of his jacket, but they were bloody uncomfortable when the holster rubbed against him. And they made him feel as if he were unevenly weighted.

To add insult to all that injury, he was a lousy shot.

He'd failed the shooting course three times. Fin had finally changed from the standard gun to a smaller sized piece, and had just barely scraped past the testing procedures.

Fin liked to talk his way through situations, to charm, cajole, befuddle or just use physical means. Turning to his gun was always a last resort and rarely even remembered, let alone used.

Preston was still staring at him, his look grim. Fin sighed and lifted his hands in defeat.

"Okay, fine, I'll carry the damn thing. And I'll check your guy out. I'll report back anything remotely suspicious."

"This could just be smoke and mirrors," Preston insisted. "I learned a long time ago that what the gossips are wagging about, or the latest new story can often be inflated if not outright libelous. You and Troy know that better than most. I'd hate to start a witch-hunt. But I still feel there's something going on there. I want you to figure it out and let me know."

Fin stood, the folder still unopened in his hand.

"I'll get onto it, don't worry. When is Marshall expecting his new bodyguard?"

"Review the files tonight and start tomorrow."

Grinning, Fin mock saluted Preston then crossed to the door and opened it.

"Oh and Fin?" Fin paused at the threshold as Preston called out again. Turning, he faced him. Preston smiled, his teeth white against his skin. "Try to stay out of mischief, at least until Troy gets back."

"Always, boss. Always."

As Fin closed the door behind him he saw Preston wince. He chuckled and returned to his desk to review the files.

Chapter One

Emily didn't know what to make of it. Keyton Marshall sat in front of a market café, sipping a frothy cappuccino as if he didn't have a care in the world. He was wedged between two men at a small table, both speaking earnestly to him, seeming to pitch something. All three of them reeked of upper class, perfectly bred business men. They all had near-identical clean cut looks, well-tailored three piece suits, polished-to-a-sheen shoes and even matching briefcases.

It wasn't a stretch of the imagination to see each of them coming out of similar molds. The best schools, happily married with two point three children and the beloved family pet.

Was there some sort of secret handbook she'd missed out on?

Keyton listened politely to the two gents and didn't appear at all bored. With his dark brown hair, brown eyes and thin-rimmed glasses, he seemed like almost any other businessman. Had she not known the power he wielded from his close connection to the Prime

Minister she'd have thought him another banker, accountant or generic—albeit well-to-do—working stiff.

The pair appeared almost to tag team him, one picking up the thread the moment the other closed his mouth. With identical hand gesticulations and matching eager looks on their faces, Emily bet it was a major deal they were trying to pitch.

She'd almost come to the conclusion that Keyton wasn't involved in selling secrets. But some inner instinct held her back from making a firm call on it. This was the fourth day of her following him and she couldn't put her finger on what gnawed at the back of her mind. Marshall worked long hours in his office according to the tiny tracker she'd managed to hide under the lapel of his jacket.

Despite the late hour of his arrival home, every night this week she'd followed him. She'd witnessed the nightly ritual of him being greeted at the door with a steamy, loving kiss from his pretty wife and being climbed all over by dressing-gown clad children. Research had taught her that the son and daughter were six and two respectively, and that his wife of nine years seemed to genuinely love him and relished being a professional housewife.

Emily hadn't been able to find any extra discretionary funds. Nor was there a hint of a mistress—male or female—whom Keyton kept in style. Indications of hidden tax benefits such as a beach house or real estate under a different family member's name also turned up negative. While financial auditing wasn't her forte, she'd become good at uncovering the simpler and more common methods of hiding untaxed assets.

Marshall didn't fit any of the molds she was used to.

Many things held Emily back from calling James and accepting the job, but the most important was she believed in her own, personal, code of ethics. She had never yet killed an innocent person. Adhering to this code had become particularly important to her in the last few months as she questioned her actions.

One of the few things that had kept her going was the knowledge that she only killed those who deserved it. This was what helped her remain strong while she struggled with her doubt. Never once had she questioned the rightness of what she did.

She didn't kill innocent people.

Ever.

The weight of doing such a thing would eat at her soul, destroy her slowly but surely. That sin would never be washed from her hands and would devastate her spirit more than anything else she could conceive of.

But Emily couldn't figure out exactly what was going on here. Why would James send her after this man if he wasn't selling secrets? James knew she tailed her subjects, surveyed them thoroughly and vetted every aspect of their lives. She never jumped in, accepting the money and killing without regard for her own beliefs. Emily couldn't understand why James would send her after someone whom he wasn't sure of.

James knew her well enough to know that if she found no evidence against the target, she'd never go through with the contract.

So why put Keyton Marshall in her sights in the first place?

Sure, she'd heard the rumors. The gossip mill was in overdrive about Marshall right now. But in a week or two there'd be some poor other idiot in their sights, accused of dirty deals. Then there'd be another person after that, and that. It was common dealings in politics.

Was James getting blasé? Thinking she'd believe a few whispers from jealous competitors and his pleas over her own research and mind? Or was she getting jaded? Cynical? Or even tired, losing her nerve and not wanting to pull the trigger when needed?

Emily struggled to understand the situation, the variables not coming together and gelling as they usually did.

She turned toward the fruit stall and picked up a ripe, fresh melon. Emily lifted it to her nose then sniffed it. Her mind remained on her inner thoughts and far away from the globe in her hands.

How could she break this seeming deadlock?

Glancing over her shoulder, she caught a glimpse of pale, blond hair. The breath caught in her throat. She did a quick double take. The man who captured her attention was tall and lanky with a head full of long hair cut to frame his face. When he turned, she noticed a quick flash of the most beautiful blue eyes she'd ever seen.

Emily knew with certainty something didn't add up here.

She'd seen this man in Marshall's vicinity three times now. Thrice in four days. She wasn't sure exactly what it meant, but she no longer believed it was a coincidence.

The man wasn't dressed for subtlety, he didn't blend into the background. With a snazzy royal blue blazer, khaki slacks, a cream shirt and a multi-colored silk scarf knotted casually about his neck, he looked like the quintessential yuppie on the prowl. Emily angled her face away and pretended to study the fruit still in her hands. Her mind whirled feverishly. Anyone could feel a steady gaze upon them and the last thing she wanted was to capture this man's attention.

Was he a political competitor of Marshall's?

Emily stole another fleeting glance. Marshall sat, oblivious to anything except the two men still eagerly chattering to him. Beside the café was a bakery then next to that a used book store. The blond appeared deeply interested in the small display of discounted paperbacks stacked in a box next to the entry to the bookshop.

No, Emily thought, *no political man would trail around after another like this. That's what lackeys and assistants are for.*

But this man exuded power, confidence and money. It was in the set of his posture, the casual, arrogant tilt of his chin and the way he surveyed those around him. It screamed 'I belong here, doing whatever the hell I want. I dare you to question my right to such.'

This was no lackey. Neither did Emily feel this man would be involved in anything as mundane as political one-upmanship or backstabbing for the hell of it. She narrowed her eyes, studying him carefully for a few seconds before ripping her gaze away again.

Her heart sped up as he lifted his head mere micro-seconds before she averted her eyes. Keeping her head down, she turned her chin to the side as if seeking a better melon. She replaced the one she held, then lifted another at random. With studied casualness, she tapped it with her index finger and raised it to sniff.

She forced herself to count slowly to five, resisting the urge to glance once again at the handsome man. Her entire focus on the fruit, Emily put it back with the others and sighed as if nothing had measured up. Emily turned and reached for an orange in the neighboring crate. She lifted her head, pretending to take stock of her surroundings and managing to steal another look at the blond man.

He seemed to be surveying the street and stores in a frighteningly efficient manner.

Is he a bodyguard?

There was something professional in his manner, something she hadn't seen from him before. Like a switch being flicked, he once again appeared to be nothing more than a fop out on the prowl.

What the hell?

The day before yesterday she'd noticed him during Marshall's lunch break. Eating at a fine restaurant at a well-sought-after window table, Emily had easily been able to find a seat at a small patisserie and watch her quarry. The only reason she'd noticed the mystery man had been because her feminine radar had jangled at his familiar face.

Unreservedly self-assured, his confidence had spoken to something deep in her. She'd admired him from afar, even indulging in a completely unprofessional, raunchy fantasy. She'd mussed that perfectly arranged hair and licked down the strong line of his neck. Emily imagined trailing her fingers over that lean chest then down his torso to discover what lay beneath those crisp pants.

Dragging her mind back, she'd memorized his features for a far more intricate fantasy later on in the privacy of her home. It'd been almost ten minutes before she'd realized what had really grabbed her subconscious attention.

She'd seen him the day before, walking a few paces behind Marshall as he left his office to head home for the night.

And now here he was again.

So that meant he was connected to all this somehow. But where did he fit in? And what would that mean to her?

Again, she thought there were far too many variables. In that outfit and the similar, over-the-top colorful bursts of jackets and ties she'd seen him in previously he was unlike any bodyguard she had come across before. So that left... Emily drew a mental blank.

Maybe he's like you? A soft inner voice whispered in her ear. *What if he isn't a colleague, bodyguard or friend of Marshall's? What if he's another assassin?*

For some reason she didn't analyze, Emily found that thought warming. Attracted to him as she was, the concept that he might be like her, that he could understand the decisions she'd made and choices she'd faced tingled in her blood, making her heat. Indulging in the harmless fantasy, she smiled and turned to feign interest in some cucumbers.

Clearly you've lost your professional edge, that small inner voice chastised her. *Cut your losses before you expose yourself any further. Text James. Decline the job. If you're weaving fantasies of a pretty face framed in blond hair with big blue eyes, it's time to move on.*

But where there's smoke there's fire, insisted a different part of her mind. *There wouldn't be these rumors if Keyton wasn't involved in something nefarious. What about that?*

Emily drew in a deep breath and stilled her racing thoughts. She'd been wrong to let James talk her into this. Turning away from the grocery stall she then walked down the street. She didn't pause or turn to look at her target as she strode past the café. Certain she was right to drop the mission she glanced one last time ahead of her to where the sexy man stood.

He turned his face, capturing her for just a second before she moved her gaze away. Even that casual exchange of utter strangers had her body reacting. Her nipples tightened, her stomach knotted lazily. Her cheeks flushed, so she lowered her head slightly.

The familiar crack of gunfire captured her attention.

For a second it was as if the entire street froze, then pandemonium broke out. Women screamed and chairs scraped back as people fled.

Crack.

Crack.

Instinct took over as the window directly behind her shattered. Emily ducked and rolled on the ground until she was half under a table. Behind her, people were scurrying out of the café and racing down the street. Marshall and his two cronies were with him as they fled, bent almost double, their hands held protectively over their heads.

Crack. Crack. Crack.

Emily couldn't gauge where the bullets were lodging, but it didn't appear as if anyone had been hit. Was this some sort of prank? A gimmick? Who shot this many times and didn't hit anyone?

Not wanting to stick around and still be present when the police showed up, Emily rose to her knees then crouched behind the upturned table. Looking quickly left then right, she assessed the easiest route and turned to run.

Crack.

The shot whizzed past, close enough that she felt heat across her thigh.

Emily didn't believe much in chance. The area was rapidly emptying but there were still dozens of people in range. The likelihood of her being targeted randomly was low, but she hadn't imagined that bullet.

They were after *her*.

Her blood cooled, her heart rate spiked and training took over. Emily pulled the long-barreled handgun from her shoulder holster. The highly illegal weapon had been concealed beneath her jacket. It fit to her hand like it was made especially for her. Emily turned to study the area around her, searching for the best sniper position and scouring where her attacker could be.

A brick wall slammed into her and she fell to the ground, winded. A masculine, woodsy scent enveloped her senses and she felt her shoulders cupped by large, warm hands.

"Are you all right, madam?" a deep voice asked her, concern in the tone. "Are you hit? Hello? Miss?"

Emily focused her gaze on the sexy man bending over her, covering her body protectively with his own. The blond she'd fantasized about had apparently decided to rescue her. She smiled, sensual heat flooding her.

He locked his blue eyes with hers, and for a moment everything appeared to stop, stilled by an intensity that burned her. His lips were luscious, full and enthralling. She leaned up, the desire to kiss them natural and instinctive. Only the sound of sirens approaching snapped her back to reality.

Screams filled the air and they both jolted as if electrocuted.

"I'm Finlay. Fin," he said, blinking quickly as if he'd been struck a blow to the head. "I'll help you get out of here, but we'll need to—are you holding a gun?"

"Uh." Emily sat up on the footpath. With a smooth motion that she'd practiced regularly, she replaced the safety as she slid the gun into the waistband of her slacks. The barrel pointed down, pressed into the hollow at the base of her spine. The position wasn't the most comfortable one, but it would take her less than a second to remove the gun should she be caught again in the cross fire.

With what she hoped would appear like a casual action, she shrugged. This moved her jacket to once more fall into place.

Emily knew it wasn't the safest way to carry her gun, nor the most subtle, but it was the carrying method she'd been taught. It was how she practiced her draw and once learned she was reluctant to change it. Besides, she was now fast and she could quickly holster her weapon when she was away from the scene.

Fin smiled at her, a devastatingly gorgeous look, making him appear like some wicked Pan ready for sensual, enticing play. As he moved back to give her space she almost missed the sight of a small hand gun holstered beneath his own blue jacket. The sirens were practically on top of them. She knew her time had just run out. Crouching, she guessed there was a small alley only a few hundred feet away. If she sprinted she should be fine and able to make her escape. She tensed her body, ready to flee.

"Ah, I've got it," Fin drawled, his manner relaxed and charming once more. "You're not supposed to carry. I might be of a mind to let you slide this one time, but I'll need to — Wait, what are you doing?"

"I'm not going to be questioned," she insisted. "I have to go."

"But I don't know your name!"

Emily turned to take one last look at his face. Her body reacted again, and she wished she was able to indulge herself for once.

"I'm Emily," she said, shocked when the words fell from her lips. On the rare occasion she gave a name while working it was always a false one, usually Amy or Sarah—common ones that sprang easily to mind. Flustered now, she half-smiled at Fin, then turned and fled.

She thought she could hear him call out to her, but the sound of the police and shouts of all the people left behind mingled together into a cacophony of noise. Emily figured it just as likely it was her imagination, wish fulfillment.

Without a backward glance and only a small amount of regret, she raced away from the entire situation. Emily couldn't believe she'd let him take her by surprise, tackling her like that. She never lost focus while she worked, she'd always been completely aware of her surroundings and in full control. If she didn't know better she'd swear the man had cast a spell over her, some sort of distraction spell.

With one heated look, a wicked grin and a bit of close contact he'd gotten her name. Damn, the man was good. No one ever said a sharp brain couldn't lurk behind a handsome face. Now she'd just relearned that lesson the hard way. He wasn't some dandified fop, but a smart, savvy man.

She needed to forget him, and the way he made her heart race and her body heat.

Swallowing hard, she tried to ignore the fact that merely remembering how his sleek, hard body had felt pressed into her slender curves made her wet. She had far bigger problems at hand. Like who the hell had been shooting, and why?

What the hell was going on?

* * * *

What the hell's going on? Fin wondered, completely side-swiped by Emily. The astonishing woman ran like a professional down the street and into the nearest alley. Fin looked behind him. Keyton and two of his coworkers cowered behind a bus shelter. All three of them were talking quickly into their phones.

A car engine revved and Fin tensed. He turned, body rigid, expecting anything. But he recognized that long, black town car and the driver. The man swerved in front of Marshall with a smooth glide of excellent steering and well-oiled brakes. The doors opened and all three men practically threw themselves into the safety of the back seat.

With Keyton being whisked to safety, Fin made a snap decision.

I'm going to catch a heap of shit for this, he admitted to himself, resigned.

Ignoring his duty, going with his instincts instead, Fin turned his back on his obligation to remain with his 'client' and adhere to Preston's mission. Instead, he raced after the surprising woman.

This isn't because she has gorgeous tits, or an arse I could nibble on all day without getting bored. There's something about her. The ease with which she held that gun, the speed of her reflexes, the fact she's here at all. It all adds up to something… I just don't know what, yet.

Fin hurried into the alley and down the long cobblestoned way. When he followed the path around the back of the shops, he caught sight of her exiting onto another street. Giving chase, he tried to not think of how glorious it'd been to feel her in his arms.

Petite but curved enticingly, she'd fit against his body as if she'd been created for him. Long, honey brown hair fell past her shoulders and eyes like melted chocolate had seared him. There was a sadness in that gaze he couldn't ignore, a weight she seemed to carry that he wanted to help her with.

She brought out the chivalrous nature in him, something he'd never thought lurked beneath his blasé exterior. He wanted to ease the pain he sensed within her, bring a spark of joy into those eyes and tease laughter from those lush lips. He craved to know what she'd look like on the point of orgasm, with all those barriers down.

Would her face be even more beautiful with the weight lifted from her heart? His mouth watered as he imagined her body slick with sweat, arching up to him in supplication as he thrust his dick deep into her glistening pussy.

His breath caught. Fin could almost feel her tight heat squeezing around his cock, milking him dry.

Shaking his head, he decided it'd been too long since he'd last gotten laid — far too long.

She's got a gun, he reminded himself. *Chances are good she's some sort of player. If you jump her, she might just shoot you instead of politely declining like a sweet, chaste little debutant would. Keep your focus, Mann.*

Fin realized she hadn't expected the shooting, however. When he'd first caught sight of her ducking for cover in front of the café she hadn't held the weapon. Indeed it had taken her precious seconds to register the danger and draw the gun. She'd been jittery, surprised.

Ambushed?

The usually silent voice at the back of his mind, his deepest instinct, floated the thought to him. Fin shook his head, discarding the idea. This was a random attack, right? Or...possibly a hit out on Marshall? No one had been after her, surely?

Really confused now, and feeling faintly guilty for chasing her instead of remaining behind to protect Keyton, Fin put on a burst of speed. His lungs were heaving and he cursed the slippery-soled leather office shoes he'd worn today. He swore, then he gritted his teeth and caught up to Emily.

Grabbing her arm, he then jolted them both to a stop. Fin quickly took stock of her. Her breaths came as hard as his, but she didn't sweat or appear unduly rocked by the physical exertion. Indeed, as he studied her, the more his curiosity was roused. She tracked her dark eyes around them both with a professionalism that shook his confidence in her innocence. Emily gave every indication of a calmness that worried him.

"Who the hell are you and what've you got to do with this?" Fin demanded more harshly than he'd intended.

"I haven't a clue what you're talking about. Let me go." She tugged her arm, but Fin tightened his grip upon her.

"Gun shots sound out in the middle of a busy city street, and you duck for cover, pulling out a nasty looking, highly illegal weapon. I can see in your eyes you're already forming some lie, Emily whoever-you-are. You're scanning the distance like a pro. I know you're tied up in this somehow. That sweet smile won't distract me a second time. What's going on?"

This time she seemed genuinely surprised by his words. He assumed the shock was sincere, as it only flashed across her face. Seconds later she'd returned to her formerly inscrutable look and frowned. Fin watched as she flicked her pink tongue out for a moment. She licked her lower lip. He wanted to follow her action, trace that plush mouth with his own tongue, but restrained himself.

While Emily thought, he wondered if her lip action was a subconscious tell on her part.

"You're reminding me that it's not just women who can use their looks to distract the enemy from thinking they have a brain," she said in what he thought was a cryptic manner.

Fin couldn't tell if her words were a compliment or a complaint. Either way, he refused to be distracted by *her* beauty. He glanced up and down the street to try to gather his thoughts. He wondered what the hell he was doing. Pulling her with him, he then stalked over to a quiet corner. He lowered his voice so they'd not be overheard by anyone.

"That doesn't answer anything. Who are you, and what do you do to justify a gun like that? What part do you play in this? How do you connect in? Is someone after you? Are you in trouble?"

"I'm not— Wait, what? In trouble? *Me!*"

She widened her eyes in what was either the best acting he'd seen, or genuine shock. When she lowered her jaw on the last word, he knew it wasn't fake. Again this loss of control only lasted a swift moment. She snapped her mouth closed and tensed. Her gaze sparked with what he could only call outrage, which further confused him.

"Is that why you followed me?" she said with scorn. "To protect me? Fin, let me explain something to you, I don't need a hero, or some man to keep me safe. I'm perfectly, completely able to handle myself, thank you very much."

Fin frowned, caught somewhere between annoyance and amusement.

"Look, just because you've somehow managed to carry around a big gun doesn't mean—"

"I can *use* that weapon," she snapped, agitated. "I'm bloody proficient at it too. Gosh, I can't believe I'm arguing with you about this."

Fin's heart thumped as she ran a hand through her hair. Fire heated in her dark gaze, lighting her from within. Emily was stunning. His dick hardened in his trousers. He gulped and tried to control himself. Sporting a hard-on here in the street would not be a good look.

"This has to involve you," he said a little hoarsely. Fin paused to clear his throat. "I can't buy the coincidence that you were walking down the street, heard gunshots and instead of running or cowering like every other person in the vicinity, you pull a weapon and start looking for whom to shoot back at. Are you in intelligence? Or with another Agency? A freelancer?"

For a moment sheer, untarnished horror crossed her face.

Shock held Fin immobile. What had he said to cause such a reaction?

"Are you?" she returned.

Fin shook his head, not following. Was he what?

"Intelligence?" she continued, clearly reading his befuddlement. "With an Agency? Oh, man. Who are *you*? You looked so handsome, so deliciously, wonderfully normal."

"I *am* normal," he countered. He felt enraged she could think him strange. It only took a moment for him to realize that, well he wasn't precisely what the girl next door might consider 'normal'.

"Well," he hedged, "I'm normal in every sense that matters."

Emily lifted her hands and pressed them against either side of her head.

"You're one of them. Aren't you? A spook. A spy. Oh shit. I need to get out of here."

Fin tightened his grip and lifted his other hand, grabbing both her upper arms, holding her firmly in place. He wasn't certain why, but now he felt even more strongly that he couldn't let her go. Marshall was safely hidden away, he knew. So while Preston would be calling him any minute once word reached him of what'd happened, Fin knew he could get the answers he craved now.

Emily was clearly upset at the thought of him working with the government. That raised a bunch of questions in his brain. Was she an illegal immigrant? A criminal? Worse? Fearfully he held her with one hand and patted her down with his other.

"What are you doing?" she shrieked. Wriggling, she tried to squirm away.

"Stop that!" He shook her, though not with much force since he only held one shoulder. "I need to know who you are, you either tell me, or I bring you back to the police. Just stay still a minute. I'm looking for your license, or ID of some form."

He ran the palm of his hand smoothly over the pockets of her slacks. He could feel they were empty. Not deterred, he dipped his fingers inside her jacket and delved into the inner lining. He found a single key—which looked like it could fit into any dead-bolt lock—a few coins and crumpled notes and an Oyster travel card.

No wallet. No purse. No ID.

Who the hell was she? And what had he fallen into?

"Look, sweetheart, I need some answers here."

"You're completely out of your mind," she answered haughtily. Jerking her arm and tearing herself free, Emily straightened her spine until her posture reeked of dignified arrogance. "I'm just an innocent passerby. Unless you're going to arrest me, I want to go."

"And if those goons were shooting at you?" he probed.

"There's no chance that's possible," she said. "I haven't done anything to warrant that kind of attack. Besides, like I said earlier, I can take care of myself. I don't need help, certainly not from someone connected with…well not from you, anyway."

Fin tried to hide the unusual hurt her words caused. He wasn't normally a person to stick his neck out for a complete stranger, no matter how pretty her eyes and smile were.

Neither was he used to being snubbed because of his work. Actually, it was usually the opposite. Women flocked to him when they found out he worked with the government, wanting to hear spy stories and thrilling tales of speedboat chases and shoot outs.

Emily was unlike anyone he'd ever met before.

Surprise, hurt and confusion had him letting her go. Silently, he watched as she turned on her heel. At that moment, however, he saw four men walking in pairs come onto the street. They were up ahead, a short distance away.

Their stance, the almost robotic precision, coupled with the heavy thud of their boots and their posture screamed to him that they were armed and well trained.

Fin reached out to lightly touch Emily's shoulder.

"Em," he warned. She jerked out from under his touch. But as she lifted her gaze he knew the moment she caught sight of the other men. She froze.

He didn't doubt for a moment that she recognized them for what they were, just as he did.

Trained killers.

Elite and powerful.

They were in deep shit.

The men caught sight of them both, their gazes honing in on Emily. They split off, two of the men picking up their pace and coming right for Emily and Fin while the other two crossed the street, presumably to come around and block them off.

"Come with me," Fin insisted. He took Emily's hand before she could utter a protest, then whirled around and ran.

For the first time since they'd laid eyes upon one another, she didn't contradict him. Fin didn't kid himself, had she wanted to stand her ground and fight this out, she could have. He laced his fingers between hers and held onto her. But they weren't glued together.

No. She *let* him lead her into a small fishmonger's just two doors down. They ran hard and fast, keeping pace easily with each other. Fin ducked behind the counter with a quick wave to the owner who let them both through with a bright grin. Fin took Emily out the back door and continued running down streets at random, weaving a complicated pattern.

He was determined to lose those men.

Only when he was sure they were alone did he pause. Impressed that she was breathing heavily, but clearly could have continued, he wondered yet again who the hell this amazing woman was. Her face glowed. She scanned her eyes across their surroundings and appeared to take everything in to the finest detail.

She wasn't some random woman caught up in all this, there was clearly more to her than that.

But no one involved in his line of work would be caught dead without their ID, even just a driver's license. Not unless they were deep undercover. Was that it? Or was she a freelancer, perhaps on holiday? No, she knew the area too well. And there was still that gun. Carrying such a weapon was highly unusual.

One other thought gnawed on the edge of his mind, worrying him with its weight.

Mercenaries rarely carried identification. People who didn't *want* to be fingered should they be caught. That thought didn't sit at all well and Fin pushed it away, refusing to believe anything of the sort. Emily wasn't like that. Couldn't be mixed up in something like that.

"Let's muddy the trail further," Fin said. Neither of them had made a move to let the other go. Still holding her hand, he started down the stairs to the tube.

Checking the signs for the next train, Emily and Fin hopped on board the first to arrive. The silence between them wasn't heavy, but Fin was unsure how to break it. He sat down with a sigh, Emily followed him. She pressed her body flush next to him on the cramped seats.

He could smell the faint apple scent of her shampoo, and the warm, musky smell that was pure woman beneath. Emily stared out of the window—she appeared deeply lost in her own thoughts. Fin needed answers. What had she become caught up in? Could he help? *Should* he help?

Not knowing where to begin and somewhat apprehensive of starting down a road he couldn't control, Fin gathered his courage and turned to face Emily.

"So do you still think this has nothing to do with you?"

Chapter Two

Emily swallowed hard. She'd been desperately racking her brain, trying to figure out what had bloody well been going on back there. Nothing seemed to fit or make the least bit of sense.

Which really, was par for the course so far today.

Fin's question bit at her. Why she hadn't ditched him at the station eluded her. Hell, why she hadn't pulled her hand free and fled the moment they'd been clear of those goons was a mystery.

She'd always worked alone. Been better off that way, too.

Emily couldn't deny, at least to herself, that she wanted to taste those full lips. Would they be soft? What would he taste like? Need clouded her brain and had her body aching. Her pussy grew warm and tingled with anticipation.

"Look, we can go back to my work," Fin suggested. "We'll be safe there. But I need you to answer my questions. If you work for an Agency yourself, or one of the other divisions then it might be smarter if we retreat to your people—"

Emily groaned softly and rubbed a hand over her forehead. Fin had been speaking in a low tone, though no one seemed to be paying either of them any mind. More than half the people in the carriage had ear buds in. Others had books and papers they read. Still, she bit down on her lip to silence herself.

In the heat of the moment she'd forgotten he was connected. She couldn't begin to explain herself. She knew practically no details about James, certainly not enough to extract herself should she tell Fin she'd been conducting surveillance on Keyton to see if she should execute him.

How did one start to discuss that sort of thing?

Besides, she was deniable. Even if she gave James' number to Fin and he called, no way would her story be verified. Those were the rules, and had always been.

She looked up as they pulled into the station. Deciding she had to go, she stood up. As she let go of Fin's hand, her heart gave a tiny flutter, a lurch of sadness.

For a few brief moments she'd felt cherished. Safe.

She'd been deluding herself.

"Em," Fin came to stand behind her as she opened the doors.

"Don't," she snapped as softly as possible. Stepping onto the platform she then headed in long strides to the exit. Fin was taller than her and had no problems keeping up. Emily gritted her teeth. She didn't want to make a scene—couldn't draw attention to them—but she didn't want him following her either. Or not really. Only a little.

Part of her didn't want to see that light in his eyes dim when he realized what she was. Emily couldn't bear for him to know how stained her soul was, how she was one of the monsters he tried to protect others from. She treasured the masculine interest he showed in her, the way his gaze made her hot and tingly. She wanted to hold onto that, not have him wrinkle his face in disgust. Turn away from her.

The station was a small one, and she'd been stalking away from the few people hovering near the stairs to the exit. When they were as far as possible from them she stopped suddenly. She turned to face him and kept her tone low.

"How do you know it's me they're after?" she lashed out. "Those shots weren't necessarily for me — it could easily have been anyone in the café."

She thought of Marshall again, and wondered if she'd been the only person told to kill him. It wouldn't be the first time multiple parties had been given the same target. She always held off, made certain the mission was one she was comfortable with, but few were as thorough as her. It was quite possible other assassins had been offered money to silence Keyton and they'd followed through far quicker.

"Then why would those men follow you?" Fin riposted. "It didn't look to me like they wanted to speak civilly, ask you delicate questions."

Emily tilted her head, acknowledging his point. She narrowed her eyes as another possibility occurred to her.

"Maybe it wasn't me they wanted. I don't work with any agency or department. I...freelance. On contract. I'm not on any records or databases. But you...you're connected to this. How do you know it wasn't *you* they were after?"

Fin opened his mouth at that, but then shut it again silently. In truth she'd been floundering, seeking to push him away so he'd leave her. In her panic, she seemed to have hit a tender place. Instantly she was remorseful.

Stepping close to him, she then laid her hand on Fin's expensive jacket.

"I didn't mean that," she said in a soft, contrite tone. "I was talking wildly."

"No. You're right. It could be I'm the one leading you into danger."

Never had she felt so conflicted, so lost and confused. Until now every mission had been quite clear-cut. Paranoia and self-doubt rarely had any place with her. But she'd been inundated with both from the beginning of this.

Looking around, she spotted a dozen CCTV cameras, as well as the Underground's own security systems. If anyone thought to look, she'd bet they were on dozens of monitors.

The feeling of possibly being watched, tracked — *hunted* made her skin crawl. Not just for her own safety, but Fin's as well. Sometime in the last hour she'd come to care for him, and now she valued his well-being — not just her own.

She'd meant to guilt him into leaving her, despite the pang it caused in her chest. But he seemed to think her words had merit. For the first time, she pondered if he might truly be in danger.

Anger stirred in her. This handsome, intelligent man couldn't be taken from her. She felt sick at the thought of him being hit by a sniper's bullet, or gutted like a fish.

Not while I still draw breath.

For the first time all week things snapped perfectly into place. She scanned the area like the professional she was. The long tunnel was not an ideal place to mount a good defense from, but neither was it where she'd try to make an ambush. The warren of corridors on the levels above them though, that was a different matter. There'd easily be a dozen places she could make a sniper's nest in.

With the multiple entrances and exits, as well as the sheer volume of people strolling around, it was an assassin's wet-dream for a hit. No one knew where they were, but they'd been standing here long enough had someone thought to send out a discreet alert for them...they could be ambushed in minutes.

"We're leaving," she said curtly, her tone blank but firm.

"Wait. What?" Fin looked around wildly probably thinking she'd seen something he hadn't.

Emily threaded her arm though his and steered them toward the exits. "We're sitting ducks down here," she explained softly. "We need to move. It's much harder to track us that way."

"Em, you're super-hot like this, all protective and professional, but I'm not convinced those guys were after me."

Emily nodded to indicate she'd heard him, but her focus remained in seeking the safest route out. On the escalators she turned her body so it would appear as if she was talking to Fin, but with her back to the wall she could easily glance above and below them and monitor any unusual movement.

A few minutes later they were out on the street. Emily had thought her heart-rate would slow when they were out of the confines of the tube station, but that wasn't to be. The street was busy, filled with people. As she scanned the area, looking for anything that gave her the sense of being off she wished they were somewhere far quieter.

Nothing leaped out at her, but it would be far too simple for even a mediocre assassin to blend into somewhere like this. Swiftly, she glanced around once more, calculating their options.

"Maybe we should go to my office," Fin suggested.

Emily noticed a double-decker bus rounding the corner. "No. We need time to sort this out ourselves, first. Let's catch that."

After jogging the short distance and weaving among the pedestrians, Emily finally reached the bus stop and lifted her hand to indicate to the driver. He swerved and pulled up at the curb. Emily noted there were a dozen or so people up on the top floor, but only a couple in the front with maps in hand. She and Fin moved to the back and sat next to each other.

The bus pulled into the traffic and continued on its route. Emily surveyed the street, finally satisfied that for now at least they'd be all right.

"I might not know everything, but you're definitely a professional," Fin insisted. "The only question I have is you're a professional *what*?"

Emily glanced up and met Fin's clear, blue eyes. Under his steady, calm gaze she found she couldn't lie, but neither did she want to repulse him. She settled for a truthful evasion.

"I deal with problems no one else can handle," she said. Her skin prickled under his watch. She looked out of the window. "When people like you find their hands tied, or unable to act because of…certain restrictions, people like me get called."

"Ah," Fin said, a wealth of meaning behind his tone. "You're a trouble shooter."

Emily smiled, though she didn't find it humorous.

"Of a sort."

"So it *is* likely those men were after you, that the sniper had you targeted."

Emily shrugged a shoulder, not at all certain.

"All I know is I don't want you killed," she admitted. "Not in the cross-fire because of me, or as a result of my leaving you to save my own skin. I know all about gray areas and understand the limitations of what I can and can't live with. It looks like for now at least I've thrown my lot in with you."

Fin lifted his arm and braced it across the back of the seat. He cupped his fingers around her shoulders, then drew her into the warmth of his body.

"Admit it," he whispered sensually, "you like me."

Emily found herself smiling, drowning in his hot gaze.

"You wouldn't believe me if I claimed temporary insanity?" she asked.

"Not a chance. You're completely focused and sexy as sin with it. You get this delightful look, as if you're readying to strap on armor, pick up your broadsword and do battle. I find it highly attractive."

Emily felt torn between laughter and embarrassment. Fin's words were light, his tone teasing, but the weight in his gaze was undeniable. Heat furled down her chest, through her stomach and pooled between her legs. Her nipples peaked, desperate for attention.

Unable to deny herself longer, Emily pressed her palm down onto his chest and tilted her chin so their lips were only inches apart.

"I'm not someone to mess around with," she warned him. "I'm...a complicated woman."

Fin threaded his hand through her hair, he danced his fingertips against her scalp. Emily caught her breath, her heart hammering. Anticipation zinged in the air between them until finally Fin shifted his face low, toward her. They pressed their lips together.

Emily fluttered her eyes shut. He moved his mouth against hers as they explored each other. Emily opened, flicking her tongue against his lip. As she'd thought, his touch was soft, his lips pliable.

When he instantly gave entrance, she rushed inside. He was as eager as she. Wet heat encompassed her tongue. Emily stroked inside, eager to explore. Fin closed his lips down over her and he sucked, the pressure shooting a thrill of pleasure along her body. She shivered, moaned and leaned in for more.

Still pressing both her hands against his chest, she absorbed the warmth from his body. It soaked through the thin fabric of his shirt and she traced her fingers in patterns over his muscles. She murmured in approval. They twisted their tongues together as they parried and fought each other sensually. He made a low sound, part groan part growl. It resonated in her stomach, the need and hunger clear from them both.

He moved her head back, twisting his fingers enticingly in her hair. They broke apart with a gasp.

"No," she panted, the cry turning into another moan as instead of leaving her hanging there Fin kissed a slow, damp trail down the length of her neck. He pressed his lips down, giving her perfect pressure, branding her skin with hot punctures. Her breaths came faster, her whole body awakening to his every touch.

She explored with her fingers, unbuttoning his shirt from the bottom just enough so she could slide one hand in against his soft, hot skin. Smoothly muscled, his lean frame was belied by a quiet strength. Tall and lanky with his outrageous wardrobe and messy bed-hair she'd have never guessed at the strong lines beneath his vibrant exterior.

This was not a man to underestimate.

"Bloody hell, I need you," he panted. Fin licked his tongue out over the base of her neck. Emily shivered, the place sensitive and highly aroused.

"Right there," she whispered, arching herself into him, begging for more.

Gently, he grazed his teeth lightly over her skin then sucked down on the spot. Feeling rather like a randy teenager again, Emily squirmed in her seat. She was wet, horny and breathless for more.

"Please," she panted. Pulling her hand out of his shirt she then pressed down on his shoulders. She lifted her torso and captured his lips with hers. They kissed passionately, tongues vying for control.

Heart racing, Emily found herself completely lost to everything for the first time in her life. She wasn't analyzing the angles, watching her back or looking over her shoulder. Her mind wasn't focused on thinking about her next step, or calculating the following move in her strategy.

She could only feel.

Fin filled her every sense. She identified his woodsy scent, something she'd forever associate with heated kisses and decadent passion. His body was smooth and strong beneath her fingertips. The sounds of the street and busy central London dimmed and only their bated breaths filled her ears.

Emily lost herself in him, let herself go.

It was exhilarating. Terrifying. Intoxicating.

The bus jarred to a halt, the air breaks huffing.

Opening her eyes so she could watch, she enjoyed the way Fin moved. Only when a family of tourists entered the bus, climbing directly up to the second level did she look away from Fin.

Reality crashed around her, shattering the shining, crystal perfect moment.

"This probably isn't the best place," she murmured, feeling reckless and dangerous.

Fin had an enormous grin on his face. He beamed, seeming proud and just as intoxicated as she.

"Who's going to pay attention to a couple of ardent lovers?" he asked, the question appearing rhetorical as he cupped her jaw and drew her face to his again.

The temptation to give in to him was huge. She wanted nothing more than to just relax and wallow in the first uncensored, unthinking moment of freedom she'd had since her teenage years.

Common sense tried to rear its head.

"People are trying to kill you," she insisted. "Or maybe me. Or hell, maybe another target."

"We're safe for now," Fin insisted. "Let's just relax and go with it. I've never felt like this."

"Neither have I," Emily admitted. She let Fin steal another kiss, the drugging intensity of it pulling at her stronger than gravity. Reluctantly, cursing herself for losing the specialness of the moment, she pulled away.

"I need to call my contact," she sighed. "I can't believe he might have set me up, but he's the only one who knew I was tracking...who could have guessed where I was," she amended, loathe even now to divulge sensitive information.

She trusted Fin, but she'd never broken her word or the confidentiality of her work. Now wasn't the time to start. Besides, it could put him in danger if he knew the true depths of what she did. The whole point of this was to keep him safe.

Or keep him near, that wicked voice inside her whispered.

"My boss didn't know we'd left the office," Fin said. "If there's even the smallest possibility it could be you those men were after I don't think you should make contact. I agree there is a remote chance it might have been me that shooter was after—but the leak of our whereabouts couldn't have come from Preston. Besides, I need to check on the man I was supposed to be guarding."

"You want to call in, but don't think I should?" She frowned. Emily wasn't sure she liked that, but tried to see the situation from Fin's perspective. She realized if they were going to stay together they'd have to start trusting each other more, even just a little. She wasn't used to working with a partner, nor being able to have someone to rely on, let alone take the enormous step of trusting.

"You phone first," she conceded. "Ten or fifteen more minutes won't make a difference to me."

Fin met her gaze and held it a moment. He seemed to understand that was as far as she'd back down, and accepted it.

"For now," he agreed.

Keeping one arm slung over her shoulders, he dug his free hand into the inner pocket of his jacket and withdrew his phone. He scrolled through his contacts with his thumb and barely a glance. Fin didn't even try to hide the number from her. Emily couldn't help herself. She caught the name and number on the screen of his android before he lifted the phone to his ear.

It had nothing to do with trust, she memorized the number because she could, and in part that was her usual practice—to take in every detail possible.

Besides, she never knew when information freely given could become useful. It wasn't in her to turn it down to spite herself or be stubborn.

While Fin waited silently for his boss to pick up, she tried to stay calm, her paranoia almost getting the better of her. If assassins were truly after him, Fin could easily be tracked by the GPS in his phone. She'd done it herself a number of times. Maybe after this she should get him to ditch it. She still had her throwaway, and there were dozens of stores in the city that sold prepaid phones and new SIM cards.

"Preston, yeah it's Mann here. I've got a situation— Oh, you've heard?"

Fin's words brought her back. Emily stared as Fin grinned wryly and fell silent. She couldn't catch every word, but she sat close enough to understand the gist of it.

"...*gunfire into a café full of innocent civilians...left him with Firth – Firth's a driver for pity's sake....my phone's been ringing non-stop asking what kind of half-arsed job we're doing...*"

Emily had to stifle a huff of laughter. She turned her head, having heard more than enough. Watching the streets flow past with interest, she gave Fin the illusion that she wasn't listening any longer.

"He got out safely though, right?" Fin said when a silence finally fell from Preston's end. "And he's no longer in immediate danger. I don't see what the problem is."

Fin paused, then shook his head.

"I can't. I've...got a few things to clear up before I can come in. I'm sorry, Preston. I'm only calling now to confirm he's back and have you check if there are any hits out on me."

"*What?*"

"After the shootout I...walked a short distance away with someone who'd been caught in the cross-fire. Four armed men came after us. There's some question as to whether this is about her, or me. I need you to check into it, please."

Fin was silent again. While she could hear the persuasive tone in Preston's voice, Emily let the words themselves tune out. She wondered what it would be like to work with someone, or a group of people, on whom she could rely.

There'd always just been her. James gave her the details, sure, and gave her free rein to work as she saw fit. But this was different. Fin didn't have only himself to trust, he had a network of people and friends who were in the thick of it with him.

She'd never realized how lonely she was, how utterly isolated her world had become. For a single, shining moment she let herself fantasize what it'd be like to work with Fin. To be encircled by his colleagues, his friends. To enter into a group of people like those with whom he worked.

You're a killer. Your only marketable skill is an astonishing accuracy with a weapon, and sharp aim. Unless they need help murdering people, what possible use would they have for you?

And as simply as that, her bubble burst.

"No. I've told you, I'm not coming in," Fin insisted, an edge of impatience creeping into his voice. "I've got...it's complicated. But I can't. Not yet. Look, get someone to dig into it, will you? I'll call you back later."

Fin hung up, tension vibrating along his body. Instinctively, Emily stroked his cheek, wanting to soothe him and not precisely sure how to go about it. It had been a long, long time since her last relationship had ended. For a number of years now she'd only indulged in flings, unable to let anyone close enough to even pretend she had room for a partner or boyfriend in her life.

Turning his head into her palm, he then pressed his lips against her skin, the contact intimate, sensual, his breath warm. Her heart stammered. The tenderness in the gesture unmistakable.

Fin glanced out of the window, bolting upright in a flash. Instantly on edge, Emily surged forward so she balanced on the edge of the seat, her feet planted firmly on the floor, ready to spring into action. She looked around them quickly, whipped her head left and right as she tried to assess where the danger came from.

Nothing leaped out at her.

Fin took her hand, threading his fingers between hers.

"My flat is only a few streets from here," he said as he pressed the call button to indicate he wanted the next stop. "Since you evidently don't want to go into my offices, judging by the look of terror on your face at the mere mention of it, we can assess the situation and discuss our options at my place."

Emily lifted her free hand to stop Fin as he moved to put his phone back in his pocket.

"Could you turn it off, please?" she asked. "And…remove the battery. I know that sounds paranoid, but it's well known how simple it is to track people with that. I'll do the same. I can call Ja…my contact from a payphone near your place later on."

Fin gazed at her for a second. Then, without a word, he switched the phone off and pulled out the battery. Emily hurried to do the same with her small phone.

"My partner says it's not paranoia if people really are after you," Fin chuckled. "I don't know which one of us has pissed off some very important people, or whether we actually have nothing to do with this at all, but right now I think being over-cautious is our best bet."

"Where is your partner?" she asked. "Why isn't she here, helping you?"

"*He's* currently in hospital," Fin said as he stood up, grabbing a hand rail for support as the bus swung around the traffic and toward the stop. "He was injured on our last mission and is recovering. Driving everyone mental, if I know him. Actually, I wish he was here. He'd have taken one look at this mess and picked out something completely random and put it all together. Or that's what he'd have us believe, at any rate."

"I've never worked with others," she confessed. "My line is…rather solitary."

Fin studied her for a moment. The intensity in his gaze burned her, in a pleasant but still searching way. Feeling as if he could see her every sin, Emily glanced away.

"Hey, it can't be that bad. Really."

Emily didn't know what to say to that, but Fin drew her flush with him and kissed her deeply. Showing him with her body what she couldn't put into words, she returned the embrace ardently. She stood on her tip toes and clung to his waist. Passion exploded between them. Pressing her breasts into his torso, Emily had never felt such lust rise in her. She wanted to strip them both naked, then thrust her wet pussy on his shaft and fuck him till they both came.

The bus no longer existed. His work, hers, the men chasing after them—it all melted into nothing and only the two of them remained.

A shudder ran through the bus and the brakes whined as it came to a halt. Shocked back to reality, again, Emily pulled away, her face darkly blushing. Fin grinned at her. He lifted his thumb and ran it over her damp, swollen bottom lip.

"There's a lot we both need to say, but it can wait until we're back at my place. Come on, follow me."

They both alighted. Emily felt disorientated, but it had nothing to do with where they were geographically and everything to do with the amazing man next to her.

Chapter Three

Fin's body was on fire. He knew logically there was no such thing as spontaneous combustion, but he didn't doubt he was about to prove that theory wrong any second now. Emily was going to drive him stark raving mad, and she didn't appear to be aware of it.

She had this way of looking around them, her gaze sharp, as if she could see and analyze everything. He knew the glance well—many of the Agents he'd worked with had a similar intensity. So how could she be so savvy, so knowledgeable and not know his cock was hard as a pole, thick and aching for release? If she'd brush those long, slender fingers of hers lightly over his crotch he'd come, in a hot mess.

She'd cast a spell on him, held him in thrall. And she was completely oblivious.

If he didn't feel her soon, find comfort in her embrace and relief in the wet, tight clenching of her pussy, he'd go mad. Utterly demented.

Opening his front door, he then stepped back to let her enter first. He supposed it appeared like a normal, gentlemanly thing to do, but he also wanted proof for himself that she came willingly with him. She shot him that small, shy smile he now craved worse than any drug, and entered his flat. Fin took a calming breath then another. He made himself pause a second, then two. He felt like a ravaging beast, the grip on his control tenuous.

After closing the door behind them, Fin watched as Emily took in his living room. He noticed a look of surprise and pleasure on her face. Emily watched him, her warm brown eyes showing genuine happiness.

"It's lovely. Colorful and elegant, just like you."

Her body relaxed, as if she'd let go of the tension that had held her straight all this time. It was far too much for him. Lust, desire and a powerful need slammed over him, carrying away what little resistance he'd clung to.

He grasped her shoulders then forced his fingers to not dig into her tender flesh. Turning them around he then gently pressed her back into the door.

"Tell me to stop if you don't want this," he growled, needing her more than his next breath.

Starved for her, Fin lowered his head then kissed her hungrily. His fringe fell into his eyes, hiding the rest of the world from him. There was only her, only Emily. Feeling like they were entering a secret, hidden part of the world made only for the two of them, Fin drank from her mouth as if this was his last moment on earth.

"Fin," Emily moaned. She arched her back and clung to him. He relished how she drew his body closer to her. He could feel the heat radiating from her, knew powerfully the need that consumed her as thoroughly as his did him.

Fin stripped her jacket down her arms and worked his dexterous fingers quickly to unbutton her shirt.

The white linen gaped and he pulled the tail from the waistband of her slacks. Catching his urgency, Emily unzipped her boots. He skimmed her trousers down over pale, lithe thighs then let her step out of the material. It remained where it lay, pooled on the floor.

He knelt between her slender legs, entranced by the tiny scrap of black lace that covered her pubes. Fin reached up to hold her breasts, restrained by a matching lacy bra. Looking up the length of her body, Fin relished the flushed, tousled and decadently feminine picture she made.

Honey brown locks framed her face, the tendrils hovering somewhere between a curl and a wave. She held his gaze with her rich, warm eyes. He saw passion, hunger and that secret knowing only a woman about to be thoroughly fucked could conjure. Her arms and legs were strong, supple with muscle. Her torso was long and lean, her belly flat and her breasts a delightful curve to her otherwise toned physique.

He'd never craved a woman more, or been so completely smitten.

"You're beautiful," he murmured. She smiled, like a goddess with a secret. She reached down and cupped his face. With her other hand she picked up one of his and guided him to cover her pussy.

More than willing to satisfy her every desire, Fin tugged the scrap of lace down to her ankles. He inserted his shoulder between her thighs to part her legs. He buried his face into her short curls. Flicking his tongue out, he then tasted her in the most intimate fashion. Wet with creamy juices, she smelled of heaven—rich, musky, salty and all woman. Fin licked her, enjoying her taste. He craved more.

With two fingers he explored. He opened her slit, her inner flesh hot and plump, fully aroused. He rubbed his thumb over the hood of her clitoris, urging it to pop out. Finding the small nub he stroked his tongue over it, lapping at it and more of her cream. Emily cried out passionately, arching her back away from the door. She pushed her hips harder into him, riding his face and fingers.

"More," she pleaded, "I want to feel you inside me. Fuck me, Fin."

"Patience," he crooned. "We have all day, all night. As long as you need."

His cock felt like a bar of hot iron in his pants. Fin had to remind himself of his own words. This would always be their first time and he didn't want to go too fast and have it over before they could explore all their options.

Wetting two of his digits with her juices, he then teased her, rubbing the pads of his fingers around the edge of her labia. Emily wriggled and cried out, urging him to penetrate her. Fin looked up at her and her dark brown gaze clashed with his. Her cheeks were flushed with need, her body taut with desire.

She hovered on the brink, clearly about to lose control.

"Do it," she insisted. "Fuck me, Fin. I want to feel you in me, taking me, consuming me."

He didn't need more invitation than that. With a small move, he thrust both fingers deep into her pussy. He panted, feeling lightheaded from the heat of his need. Her wet, tight channel closed down around him and clenched him. Emily let her head fall back as a moan shuddered through her body.

She was the most beautiful sight he'd ever witnessed.

Lost in bliss, he matched his tempo to the rhythm she set. Emily rocked her hips and he thrust powerfully into her. Fin added more fingers until he stretched her as wide as she could take him. He lowered his head, burying his nose in her crinkled hairs, eating her up. He didn't care as his face became slick with her juices, he lapped as much as he could up, drinking her as if he were a man possessed.

When he felt her twine fingers though his hair, urging him on, his heart soared. It was the first time ever he remained oblivious to how he'd look, or whether he'd be mussed or appear inelegant. A fire consumed him—burning from inside out. Only he and Emily existed, and nothing else mattered.

He felt her grow stiff, tension snapping through her body. He froze, worried for a moment he'd hurt her, touched her some way she couldn't—wouldn't—accept.

"No—" she choked out. Fin could swear his heart stopped at the strangled, desperate word. "More. Don't stop. Almost there. Fuck."

She tightened her fingers in his hair, pushing her point across. Fin resumed fucking her, his digits pressing as deeply as possible. Seconds later she trembled, straining for something, then screamed as her climax washed through her. He could feel her body sucking him, milking around his hand and mouth as he lapped her eagerly. Emily shook with the force as her body came. Fin stole a glance up at her, burning this image of her onto his brain forever.

She looked wild. Free. Part goddess and part warrior.

Emily stole his breath away. In that moment, he knew he'd lost his heart to this complicated, mysterious woman.

When she came down from her peak, Fin pulled his fingers gently out of her. He watched her, and when she lowered her gaze to his, he wickedly licked her cum from his digits, savoring her unique flavor.

"I've never climaxed quite like that," Emily said in a soft tone. The moment the words were out he saw some of her barriers come back into place. He knew then she'd not thought about her comment, it had merely slipped out.

He hated the distance he now found between them. Fin stood. After wrapping an arm around her he then held her close to him.

"That's how it's always supposed to be," he whispered against her ear. "It's just fucking if you don't open yourself to your partner. Don't get me wrong, fucking has its place. I'm really rather fond of it. But making love, that's something far more special and precious. It's only possible between people who can trust each other, who don't need secrets or walls."

Again she stiffened, though this time Fin knew it was in denial and rejection. He held her, regardless.

"I need my secrets, and I've never had anyone to trust."

"I'm not asking you to bare your soul right now," he insisted, faintly amused. "I've got far more pressing things on my mind. But what we have between us, this hunger, desire, need—whatever label you put upon it—it's special, Em. This isn't something that comes along too often. You have me now, and you can trust me. I swear. I'm hoping in time you'll choose to share all your secrets with me. But for now, I'd be happy if you share your body and heart."

She lifted her head back and they gazed at each other. The barriers weren't gone, but they'd been replaced by a wary curiosity. When she smiled it wasn't the carefree, youthful expression she'd worn earlier, but it was a good start.

"You're frightfully overdressed right now," she teased him. He smiled. Her shirt, which only covered her arms, and the lacy bra were the only items she wore. He still had everything on. Fin let Emily help strip him and in moments they were both completely naked.

"Since you searched me earlier, you know I don't have condoms," Emily prodded him, kissing him and giving him a small shove.

"Bathroom," he muttered, his brain foggy. Naked, fiercely erect and half out of his mind with lust he looked up, faintly surprised to find they were both still in his living room. "Condoms," he reminded himself, and stalked from the room to get some.

Emily could hear a cabinet open then almost immediately close, followed by the crinkle of foil. She drew in a lungful of air, not at all certain she was doing the smartest thing possible. Fin touched something deep inside her—some secret, hidden part she'd never known had been so raw and lonely.

The temptation to trust him, to join him in every way was powerful. She wanted him more than she'd ever desired another human being. If she left right now, she didn't think her heart would ever recover from being so shattered.

Yet she knew staying and opening herself further to this man could be dangerous, catastrophic even.

A part of her didn't care.

He strode back into the room and logic fled once again. Tall and lanky, his body was athletic and sensual. With his hair mussed, his lips full and flushed darkly red from his earlier ministrations and his blue gaze sparkling, he looked like a fallen angel freshly roused from a tempestuous frolic in the sack.

His cock, now covered by a thin sheath of latex, sprang up from his body, thick, long and hard. The tip was a dark red, clearly begging for relief. She'd wanted to taste him, lick the pre-cum from his tip and see how far she could swallow down around him.

Next time, she promised herself.

Fin moved to embrace her but she held out her hands.

"No, the couch," she indicated. "I want to ride you, so this time I can see your face when we both climax."

His grin was full of boyish charm, an innocence she hadn't expected and that pierced her heart. He'd spoken of them opening up to each other, but it was so alien to everything she'd learned, everything she'd become. Fin did it all so easily though. She found herself envious.

Emily followed him to the couch, her mind going crazy. She wanted him desperately, but fear held her back. Her secrets all piled up in her chest, threatening to drown her. How could she possibly have thought they'd be able to make anything together? In that instant he seemed like a mythical being. Perfect, open, trusting and free. She'd never felt more like a demon, a monster.

Fin lay down on the couch and held out his hands to her, waiting for her to climb onto him. For a crazy moment she thought about running.

"Let it go, Em," he said, seeming to read her mind. "Right now there's only you, me and this feeling between us."

Emily straddled his waist and pressed her hot core against his thick shaft. Hesitant again, she bent to kiss him. When their lips touched—exactly the same as before—all thought fled. He was right. It was just the two of them, nothing and no one else.

It was as if her earlier orgasm had been a mere prelude. Quickly her need spiked again. Her nipples were hard peaks, and this time Fin bent his head to capture them in his mouth. He cupped his hands around her breasts. He played his tongue around the tips and caressing his fingers over her mounds. Emily stroked her fingers over the smooth expanse of his chest, marveling at how perfectly he'd been made—soft skin over warm muscle, a few scars here and there adding to his appeal.

And his cock. Holy heavens, there'd never been a more perfect dick made—or not one she'd come across. Bracing herself against him, Emily drove herself into a frenzy. She rubbed her lips along his length, teasing them both unmercifully. She rode him hard and all too soon was panting. Her pussy grew slick again, her need like a fire in her veins.

"Please," he pleaded this time. The hunger in his tone couldn't be denied. Emily met Fin's eyes, amazed at how open and completely honest he was with her. She longed to trust him fully.

"Yes," she replied, not certain what she was even answering.

Circling her hand around him, she then stroked him up and down, from root to tip. He was the largest man she'd been with, but she was so worked up—damn near crazy for it—she had no doubt they'd fit. Need made her lightheaded. She lifted herself then angled him perfectly. Slowly, inch by inch, she sank upon him, claiming what they both craved.

He stretched her, almost uncomfortably so at first. They both adjusted, and soon that crawling, wriggling need to move, to fuck, to brand him as hers rose between them again. Bending over him, she rose up and sank back down, their gazes meeting.

They watched each other in the most intimate moment possible. She fucked herself upon him, and he canted his hips up to snap closed those last inches every time she sat down. Without needing words, he fulfilled her needs. She yearned to kiss him, and when she lowered her face to him, he arched up and met her part way.

They kissed—a hard, urgent press of lips as their bodies danced and sang together. Warm, wet sounds filled the air as flesh clapped together. Panting, gasping breaths sounded throughout the room. Grunts and stifled cries.

The sound of sex.

She relished the feel of one person claiming another. Who branded who was anyone's guess—they each coupled with the other on an equal basis.

Emily fluttered her eyes, but she forced herself to watch, not wanting to miss a moment of Fin's pleasure. Her oncoming orgasm grew, and soon she hovered once again on the brink.

"I'm so close," she panted, wanting him with her, now and always.

"Do it," he urged. "Fly free. I'm here, I'll always be here for you."

"Fin," she moaned, still hesitating and reluctant but unable to stop herself any longer. Emily clenched her inner muscles, grabbing his cock hard and squeezing with all her might. He shouted, his dick shuddered inside her and she exploded.

She shut her eyes involuntarily. Her senses were overwhelmed. Pleasure rocked through her like a bolt of lightning and she just had to watch this moment. Fin held her hips hard, angled her higher and thrust into her as he *poured* his own climax inside her. They grappled with their hands, bodies slick with sweat. Her ears rang, both their screams blocked out as her senses shut down for a moment to cope with the onslaught.

Milking him with her pussy, taking everything imaginable, she gave him her all. She could have sworn the world tilted on its axis, only to realize Fin had shifted. He pressed her into the back of the couch so he could pound into her harder as he rode his orgasm through to its end. She clung to him, gasping for air and stunned by the ferocity of her peak.

Drained, she collapsed into the couch and he quickly followed. It took Emily a minute or more to stop shaking, the fine, intimate tremors something she hadn't experienced in a very long time. Her first sense to return was smell. The air was heavy with the aroma of sex, semen and satisfaction. The light in the room was bright and she closed her eyes against it, wanting to take in and memorize everything about this delicious experience. Realizing she might miss something, she opened them again to take stock.

Emily had no idea how long they lay like that. They faced each other, legs entwined and chests clamped together to fit them both on the couch. She cooled down quickly, her sweat catching the chill in the air now that her blood no longer roared through her veins.

She snuggled closer to Fin, eager to share his warmth. He wrapped an arm around her. The sensation of safety and security she'd felt earlier hadn't been a fluke. She felt it again, here and now.

For some reason her body trusted him. Something in his manner, or maybe his soul, reached out and spoke silently to her.

Emily had never experienced it and didn't know quite what to make of it.

"Was it really a coincidence you were on that street?" Fin asked softly. Emily tensed, though even she could feel it wasn't the same level of force as she had reacted with earlier.

She had no idea how, or when, but Fin had crawled under her skin and beneath her defenses. There were still some things she knew she couldn't tell him—work-related secrets she felt honor bound to protect and keep—but she'd never trusted another person like she did him. Something in her instincts insisted her faith was not misplaced.

Not knowing how much she could tell him or what, exactly, he wished to know, she pondered her answer. She lifted her head and brushed her hair back with one hand. Emily met his gaze and measured her words with care.

"There was no schedule or plan for me to be there, no," she admitted. "But I was there in relation to a job I was checking on. Research. But James didn't send me to that particular café, no."

"James is your contact, the man you work for?"

Emily blinked, surprised she'd given him that but she nodded. They were both silent for a minute. She had the idea Fin wanted her to say more, but remaining silent had been ingrained upon her for so long that she didn't know where to start. Neither did she know how much she wanted to divulge to him.

"Are you one of the good guys?" Fin finally asked. She could tell he tried to put it as a teasing joke, but there was a seriousness in his eyes, a few lines of strain around those gorgeous lips of his. "At least if we're on the same side...Em?"

She climbed off the couch and turned away from him. Searching the floor for her knickers gave her an excuse to not look at him.

"I just need a second," she pleaded.

Far more slowly, with a languid grace she envied, Fin pulled himself up. He pressed a light kiss to her temple.

"It can't possibly be that bad," he insisted. "I've seen your soul. I'll clean up and be back in a minute. Then we can talk."

She cringed, not from imminent *talk*, but from his mention of her soul. Never had she felt unworthy of someone else. Emily steeled her spine. She drew on her underwear as she heard water run in a sink from where she assumed the bathroom was down the hall. Fin returned in a pair of loose boxers, looking serious but not particularly upset.

Emily shrugged her arms into her shirt and started buttoning it up.

She'd never been a coward before, she refused to start now. When the shirt was buttoned to just below her breasts, she turned around, tilted her head defiantly and prepared herself for the look of rage, disgust and revulsion Fin would no doubt wear when she told him.

"I doubt anyone would consider me a good guy, no," she started. "I shoot people. I'm an assassin."

Emily forced her arms to stop quivering, refusing to show the least weakness in front of her lover. He stared at her, his gaze steady and serious.

"Not randomly, I hope," he added with what she thought might be a faint edge of mockery in his tone. She made an exasperated sound.

"Of course not. James calls me and gives me the details of the target—he's in some branch of the government, though I've never known which covert area he's in precisely. I recon the situation, look into the target—"

"Ah," Fin interrupted. He looked satisfied, almost smug. As if he hadn't a care in the world, he flopped down onto one of the large armchairs and watched her intently.

Although she'd never had this exact conversation before, she felt lost. It wasn't how she'd envisaged it. Rage, hysterics, shouted vilification she'd been prepared for. But 'Ah' and sitting back into a comfy chair hadn't figured into her expectations for when this conversation finally occurred.

"What the hell does that mean?" she demanded, feeling decidedly off kilter.

"You did mention earlier that you were there to do research," he said kindly. Emily was still perplexed. "But I interrupted you, my apologies. Go on."

She floundered.

When the fuck had she lost control over her life like this?

"I…well. You did hear me, right? I'm a murderer."

"You mean did I understand that you've got remarkable shooting skills and no inclination to use them carelessly. You're likely contracted as a deniable operative. So when a branch of our government decides someone needs taking out and it presumably can't be done through legitimate means that person contacts you. They give you the name and after careful and—knowing you, sweetheart—thorough research, you decide whether the intelligence is correct. If you're satisfied I presume you speedily, accurately and cleanly dispatch them. Yes, I think I understand."

"I... You... But..." She didn't even know where to start with his blasé attitude and seeming unconcern with what he'd discovered. Was he crazy?

"Oh, am I wrong? Have you ever murdered an innocent person?"

"What? No! Never."

Fin grinned at her, the vehemence of her response clear to even the meanest of minds. Emily slowly sat down on the edge of the couch's cushioned seat. She peered at him, waiting for the other shoe to drop.

"You really don't mind I kill people?"

"Well it wouldn't have been my first preference of careers for a lover of mine, no," he admitted with a cheeky grin. "I'm sure it will make it difficult to introduce you in polite society. But I certainly know the need for people with your skills. There are some truly evil people out there. Do you really think I've never killed a soul myself?"

Her eyes widened. She hadn't thought of that possibility.

"You don't feel stained by it?" She blanched. The question had popped out before she could censor it. It ripped right into the heart of why she'd been so tempted to leave, to find anything else to pay the bills.

He seemed to take her question quite seriously, clearly thinking over his answer before he spoke.

"It takes something from you, yes," he admitted. "Only a truly depraved person could remain untouched by it. But these things are necessary. Most people out there, 'normal' guys wouldn't be able to begin to understand. That's why the world needs people like us, to protect the others. We keep this side of reality away from them."

She recalled he'd been protecting someone earlier this morning. That thought jingled in her mind, there was something else there, something she was missing.

"...he got out safely though...he's in no immediate danger..."

What were the chances? She'd been conducting surveillance on Marshall, Fin had been protecting someone. Could there have been two different targets in the same café?

That seemed far too much of a coincidence to her.

"If I said I'd been looking into a man suspected of selling secrets, one who was in that café, would it mean something to you?" she questioned carefully.

Fin sat upright, clearly hanging on her every word.

Funny, she'd expected a reaction from her admission of her work and got none. Now, she'd casually alluded to her so-called mission and she couldn't have got his attention sharper if she'd grabbed his arm and shaken him.

"Keyton Marshall?" Fin asked.

Emily pursed her lips together, certain now that the job had been a crap one from the beginning. She nodded.

"I should have called James and refused the job last night when I watched him read *Green Eggs and Ham* to his children." She shook her head and sighed. "I didn't see how a man who's clearly devoted to his family and clean-cut life could be selling agents of the Crown in dirty dealings."

Fin beamed at her as if she'd handed him the sun and the moon.

"What?" she asked.

He stood, crossed over and sat next to her on the couch. He placed his hands on her waist and pulled her onto his lap. Off balance, Emily turned, her thigh now pressing into his half-hard cock. She laughed, delighted but completely bemused.

"Oh yes, you're such a bad person, Em. A real hard case. Stained and tainted beyond repair." His words were filled with laughter and teasing, so she knew he didn't mean them harshly. "A woman with the courage to knock back orders she doesn't agree with. Someone who takes the time to investigate and be certain of the facts before she commits to any action. You realize it's people like you who keep Agents like me alive? You do the hardest cases we can't touch and keep our integrity. You're bloody amazing."

Emily leaned down and kissed him. Heat flared between them, threatening to consume them both again.

"I doubt Preston, or many of your co-workers would see it in the same way," she suggested as they broke apart.

"I think we need to talk to Preston, and Keyton," Fin said.

Emily frowned. "And James?"

"No." Fin shook his head. "Not yet. Let's hear what Keyton has to say for himself before we open *that* can of worms."

"Fin, James wouldn't have set me up. Why should he? I'm sure he's got plenty of people who work for him, presumably many who could kill me if he was inclined to get rid of me."

"Have you ever been to his office? Seen which division he works with? Has James ever taken you for training or seminars inside Thames House? Or Parliament?"

Emily chewed over Fin's questions. They were ones she'd asked herself before, but she had always been able to laugh off as paranoia going overboard. Her confidence shaken, she raised a hand to stop his words. She didn't want to push him further and possibly crack something irreparable within her.

For years, the knowledge she was doing the right thing had been all she could hold onto. Taking that away from her — she didn't know what would happen, or what she'd discover she'd become.

"That's enough," she said, her tone low. "Call Preston and Marshall. Set up a meeting. Somewhere public and central."

Fin glanced at the clock on the wall. Emily's gaze slid to it, taking a second, startled look as she realized it was far later than she'd guessed.

"Tomorrow morning will be soon enough," Fin said.

Emily watched her lover, letting the warmth in his eyes heat her chest once again. A few days ago she'd written in her journal how she'd felt as if her soul was frozen, her whole life cold and barren. That wasn't even close to the truth now.

With Fin, everything had come to life, including her sluggish heart and her long-dormant sexual libido. She grinned at him, an answering need building again in her belly, heart and pussy. She lifted her hands, got her fingers working on the buttons of her shirt once again. She wanted it off. She wanted to be naked with Fin.

"I'd love a hot shower," she murmured. "With you, all soapy and naked. I promised myself I'd taste you next time. I want that, to feel you fucking my mouth, all the way down my throat. Would you like to come while I'm sucking you dry, Fin? All wet and slippery, aching with need?"

His eyes burned and he didn't need to speak, his answer was written all over his face. She heard every unspoken word in the urgency with which he cradled her into his arms and carried her from the couch. Emily kissed him hungrily, losing herself in his embrace and the heat only he could give her.

Tomorrow would be soon enough to ask herself some hard questions.

Chapter Four

Emily had walked through, driven past and been over Trafalgar Square hundreds of times over the years. It'd been a long time, however, since she'd sat at the edge of the large fountain and waited, passed the time. The professional part of her scouted the area with a slow, assessing gaze, calculating angles and escape routes, finding the best sniper positions and where ambushes would work and alternatives could be instigated.

A small part of her mind had stepped back, enjoying the beauty both of the morning, but also of the gorgeous architecture that surrounded them. If it wasn't for the few bits of scaffolding that remained from the Gallery's face-lift, the scene could be placed on a London postcard and sell in the thousands.

An 'incident' that had occurred earlier in the year — one the government obstinately insisted had been a training session gone awry — had decimated most of the front façade. Except for a final column and some more delicate masonry work it had all been repaired, the damage cleaned up. A year from now, no one would be able to tell anything had ever occurred.

"Preston should be here any minute now," Fin said with another glance at his watch. Emily turned to him, a smile on her lips before she'd even finished the motion.

In a royal purple blazer, pale orange slacks and a white shirt, he made a delightfully outrageous figure. She'd snuck a look at his wardrobe when he'd been in the shower. While he did own a few pairs of regular jeans—both blue and black—they mingled with some truly amazing colors. He had trousers in all shades—green, powder blue, lemon yellow and a pair of brown cords that looked straight out of the seventies. There were also a few plain T-shirts, but his closet overflowed with all manner of brightly patterned, loud outfits.

Discreet, quiet and sober were not words one could use in describing his flair for fashion. She loved it.

"We were early," she reminded him. "I feel more comfortable that way. I can get a feel for the situation. Besides, I'm used to waiting for the right moment—occupational hazard."

"Preston is usually a little early too, punctuality is his middle name." Fin came to stand beside her. "If we're waiting on anyone it will be Marshall, though he insisted he had an early meeting that he couldn't miss. I doubt he'll keep us waiting too long either."

"Are you sure this is the right move?" Emily asked for perhaps the fourth or fifth time since they'd shared a morning cup of tea. After showering they'd raced to her home and while she changed Fin had made them both a cuppa. They'd lingered only a few minutes before catching the tube here. She'd been determined to keep a close eye on their surroundings and not be shocked again.

Being ambushed once was enough for her.

Fin took her hand, lifted it to his lips in a surprisingly elegant and gallant gesture. He kissed her knuckles. Emily's heart fluttered wildly.

"You don't have to tell him all your secrets," Fin insisted. "I'm sure we haven't yet begun to divulge all manner of intricate, personal details. We have time, years, for that yet. But I need you to see for yourself what a good man Keyton Marshall is, to hear for yourself that Preston is a noble man and not responsible for what happened. I need for you to judge all this for yourself, not just take my word for it."

"Fin..." She didn't really know what to say. She trusted him, she did, but without meaning to he was asking her to turn her back on the only thing she'd believed to be true in a world of falsehoods and deception.

"I know what I'm asking," he said, seeming to read her face.

She felt balanced precariously upon a knife edge of indecision. "You want me to tear down everything in my world, and rebuild it upon the foundations of yours," she pointed out. "That's a lot for anyone to ask of me. We've come a very long way in twenty-four hours' acquaintance, and if you were asking something smaller I'd take you at face value. I do trust you."

"I know." He grinned. "And I'm not judging you. Were the tables turned I'd need to be certain too. You're not a woman who makes decisions lightly. It's what's kept your soul intact till now. You think things through, research them for yourself and make your own mind up. No man can force your hand or bully you and I love that about you."

Emily stood on her toes and pressed her lips to his. Heat flared between them, a now familiar glow that warmed her blood.

"So you're the reckless, eager flirt and I'm the sober, serious brains. Is that how this partnership will work?" she teased.

He laughed. "I think my flirting days are behind me, sweetheart. Last thing I want is to make you angry at me. Besides, keeping up with you will almost certainly keep me too busy to have my head turned by another woman."

Emily tilted her head, coolly assessing him.

"I don't know. I bet you have a few weapons still concealed in your arsenal."

"Didn't I mention that? I'm a lousy shot." Fin winked at her as he lifted his hand in greeting to a man in a gray suit. "I practically had to bribe the instructor to give me a passing grade. Failed the test three times and was going to get booted. Bloody balls up that was— Hey, Preston!"

Caught somewhere between laughter and curiosity, Emily swallowed her questions and turned to glance in the direction Fin shouted.

A tall, dark-skinned man crossed the square toward them. His black hair buzzed short, he looked like an ordinary businessman. Emily studied him thoughtfully, then caught a few hints.

Preston searched around, showing an acute awareness of his surroundings. He tracked the other city commuters with his gaze. People were rushing all around them, going about their morning routines. The man's posture was straight and sure, balanced in such a way she felt he was no stranger to fighting and understanding the way to best use his body. Preston might be a manager now, but he'd clearly had time out in the field, getting down and dirty in the real world.

Her respect grew for him.

When he drew level with them, Fin held out his hand, releasing hers as he did so. They shook—a warm grip that appeared to be between good friends. She already knew Fin liked and trusted his boss, the ease between them showed they were mates as well as manager and colleague.

He turned those dark eyes to take her measure as Fin introduced them. Emily tilted her chin higher, refusing to cower or let anything close to her nerves show. Fin described her as 'an associate' and left it open-ended like that. While she hadn't expected him to be crude, neither had she thought he'd lie by omission.

Casting Fin a curious glance, she then quickly returned her attention to Preston as he held out his hand.

"A pleasure," he said.

She returned the firm but not tight grip as they shook.

"Likewise," she answered. "I apologize for having Fin call you out here. But...it's complicated."

"We're moving into budget time," Preston replied with a warm smile. "I'm grateful for the break. Anything not involving grant money, promissory notes, bid reports or—heaven forbid—meetings to explain and give details to classified operations I *can't* justify or give solid responses to is more than welcome. Compared to those songs and dances, I'm confident we can surmount anything you and Fin might have stumbled upon."

"Uh." Emily cast a speaking look to Fin, asking him *what now?*

"Preston, this might be a bit more delicate than I led you to believe. You see, Emily here—"

A sleek black town car pulled up, the windows darkly tinted. Emily's posture changed, she bent her knees to lower her center of gravity. She hovered her hand over her jacket, itching to pull her gun out and train it upon this new arrival. On edge, feeling exposed and under scrutiny, she memorized the license plate.

Her instincts screamed at her. She wanted to shoot and run, escape. The hair at the base of her neck prickled as she felt eyes from within the car trained on them.

"Em, it's okay," Fin whispered to her. He laid a hand on the crook of her arm. When the doors opened, an enormous, beefy security guard stood and scanned the area. She recognized the look of well-trained but hired muscle. There was no feeling of personal connection here. The guard rested his glance on the three of them for a moment, but passed on to encompass the entire area.

Despite the fact she knew there wasn't a threat here, Emily couldn't relax until she was certain. She stepped closer to Fin, unconsciously placing herself in a protective, defensive position between him and the car. If she'd thought about it, she'd have realized her posture, her natural instinct to step between potential danger and Fin was a classic symbol of someone personally involved. Although the knowledge was subconscious, it was how she'd recognized this other man as hired, not personally invested muscle.

When he'd assessed the area the man stepped fully onto the footpath and moved to make room for another man to step out of the car.

Emily relaxed as she recognized Keyton Marshall. In a similar but fresh three piece suit, he appeared calm and relaxed. Unlike her previous encounters this week, this time Keyton himself scanned the area for a moment. His glance didn't have the sharpness of a professional, but he still took the time to assess everything within the square before committing himself.

He's learning.

She turned her brown eyes to his, but no recognition shone in his gaze. Emily fought to not smile. She was quite proud that despite the complete clusterfuck of the day before, she'd still not been made by her target.

A girl needed to take what she could get these days.

Keyton adjusted his glasses, the light reflecting from the lenses. Emily tensed again. Bodyguard work wasn't her area—though being the polar opposite of an assassin's work it wasn't a stretch for her to imagine it, either. She was used to finding the weak spots in a bodyguards' defense, so that gave her some understanding. Had Keyton been her client she'd have either made him wear contacts—light reflecting from glasses was an excellent target—or she'd have him use that as a private code. Either way it set her back on edge again.

Nerves jangling, she hated being out in the open like this. She wasn't used to being so vulnerable, exposed. Every instinct in her was to take advantage of such stupid mistakes. It rubbed her wrong to be willfully indulging in such idiocy.

"Em," Fin reminded her.

The bulky bodyguard had placed a hand on Keyton's shoulder, holding him back when he would have come to meet them. Fin lightly squeezed her arm. She realized her hand still hovered over her jacket, where her gun was safely holstered, but only seconds away from being pulled in self-defense.

It took her a moment to collect herself. She'd chosen to come here, to get some answers and weigh things for herself. Yes, she felt on edge and terribly exposed, but that, too, had been her decision. Fighting her intuition she forced herself to relax, to move her hand and smile as charmingly as she could muster.

Worried about the impression she must have made, she brightened her grin and shot her best one at Keyton. The bodyguard removed his hand and the two men started toward them. Emily shot a glance covertly under her lashes at Preston Jones. He studied her thoughtfully, though she didn't feel any judgment in his gaze. Indeed, he appeared...interested. Or perhaps curious? She doubted he'd missed her reactions and hoped she hadn't blown what tattered remains of a cover she'd managed to hold onto.

"Well, that's certainly interesting," Preston said in a low tone, as if he was speaking to himself.

Keyton arrived at their small group before anyone could say anything further. More introductions ensued. Keyton looked at his solid silver watch. Emily reminded herself that her paranoia was becoming excessive when she wondered for an instant if these were yet more signals to someone outside the square, possibly lying in wait. She forced herself to get a grip. This was the stage where assassins could come unhinged, seeing meaning, covert symbols and double-crosses in every move and innocent gesture.

That level of paranoia was the tricky road upon which true madness lay.

Emily forced herself to breathe slowly. She flexed her fingers against the impulse to draw her weapon. Instead, she focused on scanning the area for hidden snipers. Keyton made an apologetic face, apparently oblivious to the trauma he caused her.

"I'm snowed under, chaps," he said as a greeting. "I can only give you five minutes, I'm terribly sorry. But Preston insisted this was important. Is it about that debacle yesterday?"

An itch formed at the back of Emily's neck when both Preston and Fin turned to her, clearly expecting her to speak. Tact and diplomacy weren't her strong suit. For a moment she was silent, flummoxed.

Keyton followed the other's lead and looked at her, waiting.

Mentally shrugging, Emily bit the bullet. She was a free agent here. She answered to no one — to hell with being polite and subtle.

"There's a lot of talk in certain circles, Mr. Marshall, that you're selling secrets." Emily held Keyton's look and tried to speak in a neutral tone. "It's been suggested since your reputation is above reproach that you'd be an ideal candidate to...play both sides of the fence — so to speak."

There was a heavy silence for a minute. Emily ignored her need to scan their surroundings, violated every aspect of her training to remain aware and held her gaze steadily with Keyton's. If she was going to accuse him of being a traitor, the least she could do was meet his look and tell him to his face.

Small lines of strain bracketed Keyton's mouth. He didn't fly into a rage, or denounce her and bluster. Emily felt her respect for him notch up. Many men in his position would posture and bully their way through such an accusation. The fact he took her words in, considered them and didn't lose his temper showed what a rational, calm man he was.

He showed her the courtesy of taking her seriously.

"That's quite an accusation, Madam," he replied. "Is there evidence to back this up?"

"No, sir." Emily shook her head. She took care to reply in an equally formal and polite manner.

"Then who are you?" Keyton asked.

"My name is Emily, sir. I'm merely looking into the situation. I'm…an independent party."

"Independent, eh?" Keyton threw a speaking glance to Preston.

Preston appeared to understand whatever was in the politician's look, but Emily couldn't translate it.

"Let me tell you something, Emily," Keyton continued. "I could sit here for hours, wasting both our time and expounding upon how much I love my country, how loyal I am to the Queen and everything our nation stands for. I could show you photos of my beautiful wife, two picture-perfect children — who incidentally, behind closed doors, turn into identical hellions when bed-time is mentioned — and wax lyrical on rhetorical gibberish and ask why I'd risk the so-called perfect life for something as base and meaningless as power or money. But I won't. What I will tell you is this. The Prime Minister and I went to school together. We joked around and pulled a few discreet pranks. We weren't caught in most of them and were never expelled. We played cricket together, snuck beer into the dormitories together and grew up practically in each other's pockets."

Keyton paused. Emily studied him carefully. When he smiled, it was genuine and full of remembrance of a happy, more carefree time. She was used to sizing people up, trusting her assessment of character. Keyton Marshall was being fully honest and seemed completely genuine.

"I don't pretend to know what you do," he said, "but in my line of work, friendship—real, honest friendship—doesn't come easily. It's rare enough, and precious enough that it's worth more than gold or all the power in the universe. Men like myself, like the Prime Minister, we don't have many friends, not the proper kind. I'm not puffing my ego up here, I'm not the only friend the PM has, nor is he mine. What I'm pointing out is there is very little on this earth that could convince me to turn my back not just on my country, but on a man I hold in such esteem as I do him. I thank God that I haven't been placed in a position where I need to make such a decision and I pray I never will. Does that help answer any questions you might have?"

Emily forced herself to take a breath and think. In her heart she knew what her next words would mean. If she accepted his answer and let this drop, it would mean she was stepping off the path she'd been on for years. That was a momentous decision for her, and one she didn't take lightly.

"Yes," she released a pent up breath with that single world, knowing her life was going to change from this. "Thank you, Mr. Marshall, I think I understand now. Thank you for your time."

Keyton smiled at her. Although she knew he couldn't possibly know what she was, or what had come so close to occurring, there was a sharpness in that dark gaze she'd not seen previously. A whisper of intuition had her wondering just how much he really comprehended about this entire, convoluted situation.

He looked at his watch again, his grin both friendly and apologetic.

"I really need to get moving," he said as he held his hand out to Preston. Keyton shook each of their hands in turn, continuing, "Judy insists I'm useless before my third cup of tea and there's this bloody budget meeting starting at nine. She sent me off with my second in a travel mug, but if I don't review these reports and get there on top of my game — well, you know how it is."

"Thanks for your time, Keyton," Preston said.

Keyton waved his hand, dismissing it as if it was nothing.

"I'm glad to see you're finally contracting people who can look objectively at problems and be direct in creating solutions." Keyton turned his gaze back to her. Emily tried not to frown, surprised he'd assumed she worked for or with Preston. She'd said she was independent, hadn't she?

"So much of our world is full of paranoia and cloak and dagger rubbish," Keyton agreed. "It's refreshing, Emily, to face a challenge head on. Much of the world of espionage is still obfuscated even to those who wish to assist it — and necessarily so — but I'm pleased to see you understand how at times the direct approach can save everyone time and effort. If I can be of further assistance to you, please don't hesitate to get in touch with me. Preston has my details. Good day."

Emily watched, stunned, as Keyton returned to his car, his bodyguard shadowing each step. He turned his head continuously, seeming to be finally aware of just how many sniper positions were available around the square. As soon as they were both in the car the driver started it and pulled away.

"Well, Keyton seems to have taken quite a shine to you, but then he always has been a savvy judge of character," Preston said with a smug air. Emily turned to face him, astonished.

"How can you possibly say that when you know nothing about me?"

"My dear girl, I haven't always worn this restrictive suit. I was out in the field making snap judgments and spur of the second decisions where you were still in the nursery learning your ABCs."

"I strongly doubt I was quite that young," she chuckled. Unless he was an unusually well-maintained man, Preston Jones could hardly have ten years on her.

Tilting his head, he gave her that one.

"Very well, but my main point still stands," Preston insisted. "Keyton saw, as I did, that you're an intelligent woman with a well-contained ruthless streak. You don't make hasty decisions and you collect data before deciding on a thought-out and informed judgment call. Regardless of your other business, you're not some hot-headed young hoodlum, you aren't easily led and I'd bet my last ten quid you've got a serious stubborn streak."

"My other business?" Emily laughed hollowly, feeling raw. Except for James, no one in the last five—hell, ten or more—years had appeared to get such a good grasp of her character or cut so close to the bone of truth. Now Fin, Keyton and Preston had all appeared to sum her up on next to no exposure. Was she losing her edge? "My other business, Mr. Jones, is that I'm a damn good shot and one of the best assassins around. Or, I thought I was. Until today, I also thought I wasn't such an easy book to read."

"Oh, you and Fin here are mere infants in this industry," Preston assured her with a smile. He didn't seem the least perturbed, nor surprised, at her reckless confession. Who said she couldn't be goaded? "You're thirty?"

"Twenty-nine," she admitted. He chuckled.

"Yes, definitely a good match. Finlay is thirty, and I'd been quite concerned about him settling down. Anyway, I know you two have plenty to discuss, so I'll leave you to it. Oh, here's my card. Should you ever decide to broaden your horizons, please give me a call."

Emily took the card and frowned. She knew that she should feel pressured, but Preston's words and manner were so casual, as if he couldn't care less whether she took him up on his offer or not, she wondered if she misread the situation.

"I have thought about broadening my horizons," she insisted. "And I have some mild talent at journalism. But truthfully, Mr. Jones my only real skill is in shooting people. What possible use could you or your Agency have for me?"

Preston grinned, shook Fin's hand and turned back to her.

"Miss Camber, do you really think we don't have need for the occasional shooter? Sometimes — they're not frequent, but they do pop up now and again — there is no alternative except to kill certain individuals. As I'm sure you're aware there are people simply that evil, or situations that dire. I can think of a dozen missions this last year alone where it would have been extremely useful to have someone of your skill along as a last resort. Don't fool yourself, there are more people like you around than you'd believe."

With that, he exited, leaving her surprised and incredibly thoughtful. Fin wrapped an arm around her shoulder and she leaned into him, relishing his strength and warmth. Despite the weak sunshine trying to filter in through the light clouds, she felt quite cold suddenly.

"That went quite well," Fin said, breaking into her reverie.

Emily looked up at him. A huge grin crossed his face. She felt her heart catch. She lost herself in his blue gaze, feeling warmed as if the sun had come out again merely upon his say so. Lifting herself up, she then kissed him, releasing the tension that had been tied up inside her all morning.

After turning in his embrace, she moaned as Fin closed his arms around her, holding her tightly. They pressed their bodies together and she canted her hips up. His body exuded heat and she enjoyed the knowledge that their touches built passion in him as well. That it wasn't just *her* loins stirring. A car beeped and she jerked, recalled back to reality with a crash. Once again she felt the back of her neck itch.

Emily no longer cared whether it was paranoia or just plain idiocy, she felt compelled to move. It wasn't in her nature to remain so exposed and she hated the feeling of being vulnerable. She couldn't sense any immediate danger—perhaps she was deranged—but she'd ignored her instincts for as long as she could manage.

"I need to think," she said as she reached out and took Fin's hand. Seeming content to follow her, he put up no resistance and let her lead him down the busy street.

Chapter Five

Hand in hand, they silently walked down Pall Mall. Her head was full of conflict. Emily couldn't think of a word to say. As they came to St. James Square, the greenery in the middle of the busy city called to her. Emily paused, Fin followed her lead. She scanned the park, finding a number of more secluded pockets. Without letting his hand go, she took them to a grassy area shaded from three sides of the square by some large hedges.

Finding a good defensive position, she then checked the ground to make sure the hint of morning dew had dried. She sat. Hidden from anyone not coming directly toward them, and with Fin's lanky form spread casually next to her, their thighs and shoulders pressed together. Emily felt safe, secure for the first time all morning.

The rush to get to work had abated, only a few casual strollers here and there. While the park wasn't empty of people, Emily convinced herself she and Fin had at least the illusion of privacy.

"I really don't want to think about this," she said, knowing it had to be done. Fin nudged her shoulder with his arm, somehow managing to convey comfort and solidarity with her while wearing a cheeky grin.

"I can't imagine you're the kind to shy away from difficult things," he insisted. "You've a cool head under pressure. When those snipers were having a go at you, you didn't cower or wait to be saved, you had your gun out, crouched and looking for ways to retaliate. You've a warrior's spirit."

"Physical action is different," she demurred. "You know what it's like. Adrenaline pumping, fifteen things going through your head at once, and somehow your brain rises above it and can see the world with crystal clarity. Instinct takes over. This is…emotional, and messy. Painful."

The final word was practically a whimper, and she hated that. Loathed the small, hurt sound that came from her. Part of her wanted to curl into Fin, touch him, lick him and ignore the rest of the world. They could lose themselves in each other, use the sexual chemistry and heated passion that grew between them to shove the world far, far away.

Had he reached for her then, she'd have thrown caution to the wind and indulged in the intoxicating chemistry she found with him—to hell with good sense. They'd have both been arrested by the first policeman to come around the corner. Emily wondered who she'd be able to call to bail her out.

With a strangled groan, she realized just how very isolated she'd been.

Was this what it had all come to?

"Hey, you'll be okay." Fin rubbed the palm of his hand up and down her back in a soothing and oddly chaste gesture.

"I just realized I have maybe a dozen friends, people who until now I thought I could call on if I needed help. But if I was arrested right now for public indecency, for jumping you and fucking you like crazy right here and now, there is no one to whom I could explain that."

For the first time since she'd met him, Fin appeared struck dumb.

Blinking back tears that threatened, she turned to him with a sad laugh.

"Do you know you're the first person I've ever told what I do?" she said. "You're the only one who knows my real work, and somehow, miraculously, understands? You don't judge me. And now Preston, who somehow thinks I might be useful. Even Keyton—the man doesn't even seem to know a thing about me, but he gets the situation. I completely understand what he means by having friends like that, their value. He'd suffer torture before turning his back on that."

"Everyone has a weak point," Fin pointed out.

She nodded. "Of course, and I bet if someone took his wife, or children, he'd be forced to make that decision. But it would break him and forcing him that ruthlessly would destroy the power and use he holds. But that's not my point. I believe him. He'd never willingly deal under the table. So that leaves me with a larger problem."

"James."

"Exactly. He knows my standards, knows I take them seriously."

"Have you turned jobs down from him in the past?"

"Yes, twice. Both times he had faulty intel. The first time was my fourth contract. I always thought he was testing me, wanting to see for himself if I'd turn him down. The other was only a year ago and I think that was a genuine mistake—he'd been given bad information and acted rashly."

"Mistakes can happen, but they're extremely costly in this business," Fin said in a soft tone.

Emily couldn't meet his eyes, staring instead at his bright slacks and running her hand idly up and down his thigh.

"I know. That's why I take my part in it seriously. Not questioning orders can be soul-crushing. I've never let James think otherwise. But I've always assumed for the less clear-cut contracts, he'd have others on hand. Why call me when he knows it's a real possibility I'll refuse to do what he wants?"

Fin was silent for a moment. Emily lifted her gaze and watched him. Shaking his long fringe from his eyes, he made a puzzled face and shrugged.

"I can't answer that. I really don't know," he confessed.

"What possible reason would James have to kill me?" she demanded, hurt and confused. "There's nothing special about me, no risk that I can be to him. Hell, he didn't even know where I was. He couldn't have arranged it. I'm clearly becoming too paranoid."

"He knew you'd be following Marshall, right?" Fin said.

Emily paused, then nodded. "Sure, it was a safe assumption. He knows I follow my targets. That's never been a secret."

"So if James had access to Marshall's whereabouts, it would be simple for him to know your position. Marshall and his mates had been lingering over their coffee, we'd been at that café, what? Twenty minutes?"

Emily thought. A nasty, crawling sensation over her skin made her feel sick as too many pieces of the puzzle fit together. She wasn't liking the picture she saw.

"Okay, but he'd need to know where Keyton was."

"Those rumors have been circulating for weeks," Fin added in a gentle tone. "The whispers are still quiet, but ears have been listening. Keyton's reputation is solid, practically above reproach. But that doesn't mean others don't want to jockey for his position. He's been under scrutiny—delicately, subtly, discreetly, but still under close watch. I bet there'd be many people who had access to his schedule, who made note of when he leaves and enters the building. If James really has the connections you believe, I'm sure there'd be any number of palms he could grease. It isn't a stretch to imagine he could know where you'd both be and set something like this in motion."

Betrayal cramped in her heart like a physical pain. Fin seemed to read the realization on her face. He cupped the back of her head, tangled his fingers in her hair and caressed her scalp. Pulling her close to him, he then kissed her hard, as if to heal the wound she felt.

"I'll kill the bastard," he whispered. He licked his tongue along her lower lip, heat from his mouth soothing as much as the scattered kisses they strung together. "I don't know why he'd do something like this, but I'll gladly shoot him for it."

"I thought you were a terrible shot?"

"I'll practice, I have incentive now."

She chuckled, the feminine part of her pleased for his protective nature.

"We don't know for sure he's behind it," she reminded him. "And I like to be certain of these things. Come back to my place, I need time to think and mull this over."

Fin gazed steadily at her, his look searching.

"We can get something to eat around here," he suggested. "There are plenty of decent places for brunch. I'll pay."

Emily shook her head and glanced around them.

"No. I feel more secure here, but…I'm not sure if my instincts have been altered from my heightened paranoia or if perhaps I really am losing my edge. I'd rather be behind closed doors."

Fin stood and held a hand out to help her up. She twined their fingers together, leaned against his chest and pressed their bodies flush as she whispered against his lips.

"Besides, there are things I can do to you back home that a good girl would never dream of doing right here in the middle of the park. Naughty things."

"Naughty things? Really?" he repeated, clearly intrigued. "Well then, lead the way, sweetheart."

* * * *

Steam filled the room, billowing in the draft created by the open bathroom door. Emily ducked her head under the hot spray and imagined washing her troubled thoughts down the drain with the water as it sluiced down her body. Tilting her head to the side, she strained to listen above the hiss of the shower.

"Are you coming?" she raised her voice, startled as Fin's lanky shadow filled the doorway.

"Not yet, but I hope to," he replied as he opened the door and stepped into the stall.

Emily looked down the long length of his body, licked her lips at the delicious sight he made. Moving to the side, she shared the hot water with him, pleased she'd invited him in. Fin placed a foil square onto the small shelf where she kept various products, then winced a little at the temperature she'd set the spray to. He reached out to catch some water, then moved away quickly. Testing the temperature again, then again. His actions were timid, like a kid dipping his toe into the ocean, needing to gird himself to fully committing.

She threw her arms around him and laughed as she pivoted, dunking him beneath the faucet. He shouted in protest, but then let the water pound against his head and drip down his body.

"It's always easier to jump right in," she teased. "Like ripping off a bandage. Going slow only increases the pain."

"I was acclimatizing," he insisted.

She grimaced. "You were dithering."

Fin pushed them both forward, pressing her back against the cool, slick tiles. They fused their lips together and passionately kissed. Emily lifted her leg, wrapped herself around his hip and clung, her body and soul opened to this amazing man.

Water poured over them, steam filling the small cubicle and making it seem as if they were on their own plane of existence. Fin stroked the side of her face. He traced the pad of his index finger in a slow circle at the base of her collarbone where she was sensitive. She shivered in delight. Gaze narrowed, heat flared in his pupils. It made his eyes appear darker.

He brought his free hand around to cup her arse. He kneaded the globe and pulled her cheeks apart lightly and ran his fingers over her puckered hole. She squirmed, excited but also hesitant. That wasn't an activity she'd ever indulged in.

"Shh," he whispered, kissing down her neck. "Later. Not now."

She relaxed, her body arching into him. Emily tightened her leg around his waist and canted her hips up. She could feel Fin stroke over the thin, tender skin that ran from her anus down the curve of her buttock. Wandering his fingers around, he made a slow progression to her labia. He pried with his index and middle fingers, then opened her fully to his touch.

Sensitized, she moaned as the pad of his digit woke her clit. Sweet energy raced over her, heightening her pleasure and blossoming through her blood. Need hummed through her like the tune of a well-loved song. Emily lowered her head and pressed a hot kiss to Fin's chest. His brown nipples were erect. She flicked her tongue over them before capturing them and sucking him. He hissed out a breath, caught by surprise. She drew on the tender flesh, licking him and sucking again.

She knew it wasn't the same experience she felt, but just as many nerves were present on a man's chest as a woman's.

Caught up in the erotic moment, she enjoyed watching Fin stretch, then arch his spine. Power rushed to her head, intoxicating and potent. She recalled her earlier promise to herself. She lowered her leg and grabbed a hold of each side of his waist. Emily knelt on the slick, wet tiles then kissed a languid, meandering trail down his torso, over his left hip-bone until her lips parted at the delicious discovery of his large, wet cock-head.

Opening wide, she encompassed his tip, licking along the slit and tasting his salty essence. Fin groaned. He fisted his hand in her wet hair. She shifted on the base of the stall to give herself better balance. Emily nudged him with her thigh, urged Fin's back against the wall. He spread and bent his legs to the perfect height for her.

She circled her fingers around the base of his shaft, then twisted with a screwing motion. Sucking his tip she then licked him and bobbed her head. She palmed his balls with her other hand, then stroked against the tender skin.

"Oh fuck, yes. Just like that, sweetheart."

She enjoyed caressing him and the fullness of sucking him deep into her mouth. Water mingled with his salty flavor and her hair clung to her back and neck. She hummed, wanting the vibration to add to his pleasure, then sucked harder as she continued to move her head up and down. Fin tightened his fingers and a small gush of thin pre-cum splattered against her tongue.

Encouraged, she pumped her hand up and down his shaft, pressing against his warm skin and stimulating his cock. She played with his head, sucking the tip. Emily relaxed her jaw and lowered herself as far onto him as she could manage without choking.

"Oh yeah, oh hell yeah," Fin groaned, his shouts louder this time as his pleasure grew. She mumbled, her own body hot and aching with need. Fin's thigh trembled near her head. He clasped his hands into her hair, urging her to move down lower. She could taste the fluid as his cock prepared for climax.

Her heart sped up, racing as she readied for him to come pouring down her throat any second now. Then Fin took her completely by surprise.

"No, I want to be inside you," he groaned. Emily had barely heard the words when Fin tilted her chin, then pulled her under the arms, lifting her up onto her feet.

"Fin," she panted, still in a state of shock.

Quick as lightning he turned her around. Her breasts and torso pushed into the slick, wet tiles. She heard a crinkling sound and managed to throw a look over her shoulder to see him sheath himself. When Fin reached between her legs, she knew she was wet and more than ready for him.

"I want you just like this," he whispered in her ear. He pressed his chest into her back, then aligned his hips with hers. His crotch pushed into her arse and she instinctively ground back onto him. He closed his large, masculine hands over her hips, tilting her pelvis just so. In a long, smooth motion he dipped and his dick slid straight into her pussy.

"Oh," she moaned, her voice wobbling as a million nerves ignited into life. He penetrated her more deeply from behind, his thick cock running over every sensitive place inside her body. They groaned and he withdrew. When he pushed back in, harder this time and faster, it was as if the world imploded.

Emily lifted her hands, rested them against the slick wall and pushed her hips back into his possession. Fin tightened his grip around her pelvis, but she didn't care. He canted her hips higher, moving with more force inside her. She cried out, both in pleasure and awe, the exquisite sensation bombarding her now.

"More. More. Please," she shouted, incoherent with lust.

Fin pounded into her. Water sprayed everywhere and the wet slapping of their flesh filled the small bathroom. Emily flexed her fingers, grabbing for her climax as it hovered just beyond her reach.

"Almost, almost," she panted, strain in her tone tinged with frustration.

She was so close, but she couldn't quite make it.

Fin reached down, sliding between her stomach and the wall. Lower he moved, until he came between her splayed legs. When he rubbed his finger over her clit, it sparked a new fire, stealing her breath and sending her over the edge.

She screamed, instantly catapulted into orgasm. Her body tightened, her pussy contracted, squeezing around his driving shaft. Wave after wave buffeted her, pleasure shooting through her body. She shuddered and closed her eyes to better feel the sweet release.

Moments later Fin shouted, his hips snapped forward, thrusting her into the wall as he pumped deeper into her. With their bodies squashed together, she enjoyed the raw intensity of his orgasm, so similar yet different to her own. Her legs wobbled and she was pleased his grip remained on her waist and his body pressed along hers. She could have easily sunk to the floor, a mindless, quivering wreck.

They each caught their breath. Finally, Fin carefully, tenderly pulled his cock from her body. Emily got her bearings and found her feet, turning to push her back into the wall and stare at her lover with what she hoped wouldn't be a soppy smile.

Without a word, Fin ran his hands gently over her, then cupped the water and rinsing her body. Together, slowly and with an air of casual intimacy, they cleaned each other from their passions.

Chapter Six

Emily turned the kettle on then stared sightlessly out of the kitchen window. Still damp from the shower, she had wrapped her robe around her and promised Fin tea when he urged her to join him in bed. Her heart felt warm and full, she couldn't believe how lucky she was to have met him. Already her life felt brighter, complete with his presence.

There were always shadows though, but this time they were of her own making. Small memories were tarnishing what should have been a time when she could bask in the bloom of her first real, honest romance. She recalled how very annoyed James had been, that second time she'd turned down his contract.

"I'll double the usual price, triple it. For fuck's sake, Emily, what's wrong with you? The man needs killing..."

She'd remained adamant, refused to kill him when she didn't believe he was truly a traitor. In the end she'd been right, the target had been blackmailed and while he had done the deed, it had been under duress, a good man caught in an impossible situation. When the truth had come out—splashed across the tabloids and newspapers, no less—she and James had never raised the matter again.

Then there was his clear irritation at her wanting to reassess her work with him.

"You're a natural, using your talents in the best possible way, what do you mean you want time to reassess your life...? We do so much good together, do you want to throw it all away because it doesn't live up to your dream-like expectations?"

She still couldn't believe James would want her dead for something as paltry as wanting to leave. Death being the only exit was a thing for over-heated novels, mafia-based conspiracy theories and the movies, not real life. But Fin's point was a genuine one. So far, it was also the only even remotely logical reason she could think of for James wanting her dead.

The kettle boiled, drawing her attention away from her convoluted thoughts. She made them both a mug of tea and returned to the bedroom. Fin lay sprawled across her bed, blond hair mussed, superbly naked and still flushed from either the shower or their earlier lovemaking. She grinned as she set their drinks on the bedside table.

Climbing onto the bed, she then straddled him. Grinding down a little and rubbing herself against his warm crotch she enjoyed the moment. He lifted his hands and in a few short motions removed her robe. He cupped her breasts in his palms, toyed with her nipples. His fingers were wicked, dexterous and played her to perfection.

A low, approving moan escaped her lips. She fluttered her eyes closed and let her head fall. Her hair swayed against her naked back.

It would be the easiest and most delicious thing ever to let him take her again. Already she could feel the slow burn of desire knot in her stomach. Her breasts tingled, her clit ached to feel his touch. Wetness gathered in her pussy and she knew she could spend the rest of the afternoon—and every one thereafter—lost in this delicious man. Leaning forward, she pushed her palms against his chest. She splayed her fingers and caressed his soft, warm skin. With hot kisses, she tasted him, licking his lips and watching his pupils flare, desire and need heating his gaze until the sparks ignited between them.

"You look delicious there in my bed," she said huskily. "Rumpled and tousled, ready for sin and pleasure. This isn't the first time I've thought you embody wicked sex like some luscious fallen angel. But I can't let you distract me again."

"You've got something better in mind?" Fin teased, his look predatory and decidedly hungry. She shook her head and sat up. Moving away, she ended up sitting next to him on the large mattress.

"Not better, sadly. I'm going to call James, tell him I won't take the job."

"Okay," Fin agreed. "He's probably already guessed, but it won't hurt for you to tell him. He'll likely be expecting it."

Emily gathered her courage. That had been the easy part. She'd wanted to lull Fin into feeling amiable, though she didn't think anything she said would soften the rest of her plan.

"I also want to suggest we meet. It's likely he'll be annoyed when I turn this contract down, it should be fairly simple for me to set up a face-to-face with him."

"Absolutely not," Fin snapped, sitting up. "Are you insane? If I'm right the man has already tried to kill you once this week. Do you want to make it easy for him?"

"I'm not stupid," she replied. "I'll take precautions. If James is behind all this he's gone to lengths to hide his involvement. Using hired thugs and snipers. He's not going to get his hands dirty by killing me himself in public, in broad daylight. That's not his way."

"It depends on how badly he wants you out of the picture," Fin said with a stubborn set to his face. Emily had to struggle to not smile. Fin might appear to the casual observer as a peacock of fashion, idle and a dabbler with more money than sense, but he could be remarkably obstinate, she had discovered. It didn't surprise her as such, anyone who worked in espionage had to be dedicated and resilient, but it made her smile to see those lush lips and gorgeous jaw set in such annoyed lines.

"I'll suggest we meet at Covent Garden Market," she tried to placate him. "James will go for that, there are a million exits and entrances, plenty of safety. I can talk him into it, I'm sure."

"That's not what I'm worried about. It's that he'll be willing to do so and use the situation to his own advantage." They were silent for a moment, both being stubborn. Fin capitulated first. "Fine. But I'm coming with you."

Emily blinked. In an instant she should have realized he'd insist on that, but it honestly hadn't occurred to her. Caught flat-footed, it took her a moment to stumble out a reply.

"There's no way James will meet while another person—a stranger to him—is present. Don't be ridiculous. You can wait here, or a few blocks away."

She couldn't say what was truly on her mind—that if James really did harbor ill toward her she didn't want Fin within a mile of their meeting. Not just because she couldn't focus if Fin was in danger, but because it would destroy her if harm came to him on her account. She couldn't live with that.

"I do know how to be covert," he insisted, frowning now. "I don't see why I can't linger nearby. This isn't my first day on the job."

Emily felt a shiver of apprehension. She had the impression he wasn't going to let this go, not without getting his own way.

Damn stubborn man.

"I'm not calling your professionalism or your manhood into question." She searched desperately for some way to get her point across. "This isn't about you. It's about me discovering if I've been used like some weapon. I need to know if I've been lied to, betrayed by the only person I thought I could trust."

"And I'm not taking that from you. But you're not alone anymore, Em. You have me. Damned if I'm going to let you walk into a trap with no backup. That isn't how I work."

"I don't want you hurt, not on my account."

Fin's face softened. He sat up and cupped her cheek tenderly.

She sighed, turned her face to kiss his palm. The anger and tension seemed to seep from the room as if he had never been there.

"Would you let me walk into a trap, possibly risk my life just because I didn't want you hurt?" he asked.

Emily's shoulders fell, the fight draining out of her. "No. Never."

"Then don't ask me to do the same. I love you, Em. I know you can protect yourself, but it never hurts to have someone watching your back. I'll keep my distance, but I refuse to let you go out there alone."

"Okay. But if he hurts you, I swear to heaven I'll hunt him down like a dirty dog."

Fin grinned. "You took the words right out of my mouth, sweetheart."

Emily lightly pressed his shoulders, pushing him back onto the bed. She followed him down and nipped a stinging, biting kiss to his chin.

"Did we just have our first argument?"

"If you're offering make up sex I'm willing to concede that," he grinned cheekily.

"I'm always up for a quickie," she purred.

Reaching down to stroke his shaft, Emily intended to ramp up the simmering lust humming between them. But she glanced at Fin. His gaze were hot, but there was also a tenderness there she'd never witnessed with her previous lovers—a kindness, a level of intimacy that made her blush.

He ran his hands over her skin, the palms smooth and his fingertips tracing lines delicately. His cock grew in her fist, and despite her previous thought of a hot, hard coupling she found her touch gentle.

They moved in tandem, the lust and hunger fiery between them, but a new tune had been added too. Fin's glance was almost adoring, something she'd never witnessed before. It made her simultaneously embarrassed and unbearably turned on. She never wanted to see disgust or hatred in those beautiful blue eyes.

He reached out and fumbled with the nightstand, then finally grabbed a foil packet. With a wicked grin she took it from his hand and scooted down his body, needing just a moment to breathe and remember they'd only known each other a short time.

It didn't matter.

Emily could feel her heart swell. She knew this love, fast as it might be, would be with her forever. She sheathed him and tried to catch her breath.

"Hey, are you okay?" he murmured. Fin gently grasped her arms and drew her back up his body. Emily gazed at him, nervous about what he might see in her eyes, but refusing to be too cowardly to face him. She smiled and remained silent.

She answered him with her body instead.

Angling his cock, she adjusted him and thrust down upon his dick. He was hot, thick and seemed to fill not just her pussy, but her chest, her throat, her very self. Emily moved on him, but what had always been a sensual method to get physical release was now filled with hidden meaning.

Fin possessed her. Not just his shaft, but Emily could sense his essence, his soul twining with hers. She shook her head. Never one for whimsy she couldn't believe the nonsense filling her mind right now. But she couldn't deny it, so much more than the act of fucking was occurring.

"Kiss me, love," Fin said.

Emily touched her lips to his and need exploded. They moved together faster and harder, their skin slapping together as something huge and unknown blossomed in her chest. Emily tried to close her mind to it, to focus on the fucking, the raw physical act.

But she knew it was too late.

She loved Fin. Wanted more with him and from him than she'd ever dreamed possible.

Desire knotted in her belly, her sensitive, raw flesh hummed as they moved against each other. And all too soon she felt that shimmering peak just come within reach. Fin stroked her clit and the world exploded. She came hard, clenching around his cock and shuddering as something deep within her broke loose.

The thought terrified her, but Emily knew she'd given him her heart.

Fin wrapped his arms tightly around her and she struggled not to cry.

He held her, not saying a word. She knew he couldn't possibly have read her mind, but just as she'd been able to read his gaze, she worried he might have seen far too much in hers. They snuggled together. She caught her breath and tried to mentally shake some sense into herself.

There was still work to do.

Emily kissed him, hot and hard. Pulling away, she then moved to the bedside table, reached past Fin's snazzy android phone and picked up her smaller, battered throw-away mobile. She yelped as Fin grabbed her naked arse and gave it a squeeze. She slapped her free hand out at him, batting him away.

"It's not an invitation every time I bend over," she chuckled, dialing James' number.

"It sure looks like one to me, sweetheart," he leered.

Emily hushed him as the phone rang.

"Yes?" James answered.

"It's Emily. I've been looking into our client and I can't find any basis for your thoughts. I'm declining."

"What? Dammit, Emily, I thought for once you'd bloody well—" James cut himself off, clearly struggling to keep his annoyance in check. She heard him suck in a breath. It didn't take much imagination to know he was reining in his temper. "Emily. I know he looks like Mr. Clean Cut from the outside, but you're going to have to trust me on this. Keyton Marshall is dirty. His image and good reputation highlight why he's untouchable. You can't begin to believe the damage he can do to our nation. He needs to be taken out."

"I don't agree. He loves this country and has far too much to lose to switch sides."

"That's part of the thrill for men like this. Look, have I ever led you wrong? You know I can look far deeper than you can into these sorts of things. You need to believe me."

"Well..." Emily pretended to hesitate a minute, her brain working feverishly. "Do you have evidence, something you can't send via email or text, but would convince me?"

"Yes. Absolutely."

"Okay, then let's meet." Emily stared out of her bedroom window at the gray afternoon, the sun struggling to shine between the clouds. She couldn't look at Fin, worried it would distract her.

"Perfect. Fine. I can do that, where are you?"

"London," she remained purposely vague, then hurried on. "How about Covent Garden Market? You've told me you often take a late afternoon stroll around there, is that right?"

There was a slight pause, but it was so brief she wondered if her paranoia was getting a hold of her again. "Yes, of course. That's perfect. I can duck a meeting and be there by three."

"I'll be there."

Emily hung up, took a shaky breath and sighed in relief. Finally, she met Fin's warm gaze.

"That was magnificent. Even only hearing your end it sounded like you played him perfectly."

"I must be demented. It's like I can see the flip side of two totally different scenarios. Either I'm about to shoot myself in the foot and destroy the only career that's ever made money for me, or James has been playing me all along and I'm the biggest fool in the universe."

"What do you mean?"

Emily pulled the sheet over her thighs and sat cross-legged on the bed. "Before today I'd have thought there was this unwritten rule between James and I. We never meet. Ever. Logic and a million reasons back up that rule, but yet it took me almost no effort to convince him. So on the one hand maybe he is trying to kill me and sees this as an opportunity. The other side to that coin is perhaps he is so adamant, so personally convinced that Keyton is dirty and selling our government out he's willing to risk everything— *everything*— to convince me of this."

Fin remained silent and she was grateful for that. He didn't try to sway her, or offer his own thoughts on the matter—just let her thoughts hang on the air. She glanced at the clock, sighed and rose to her knees. Kissing him tenderly, she then moved down so she could lay her ear over his heart. She listened for a minute to the steady rhythm, enjoying the sound of his life pumping beneath her. It soothed her jangled nerves, calmed her the way no words could have managed.

"We need to get ready," she said without moving a muscle.

"Well we could always turn up to the Market stark naked, I'm sure plenty of the patrons would enjoy the view."

They both chuckled, and Emily loved how the sound reverberated through his chest. It sounded as if a deep, rolling thing were alive within him. She promised herself that as soon as they were done they'd return and she'd talk to him all through the night, listen to his heart thump and make him laugh so she could hear that lovely noise all over again.

Sitting up, she took one last mental picture. Fin, splayed out on her bed, his hair mussed, eyes shining. He looked beautiful, perfect.

Hers.

"Okay, let's go." She climbed from the bed, mentally preparing herself for the confrontation to come.

* * * *

Fin couldn't remember the last time he'd been so nervous. He felt positively naked without his usual array of toys and gadgets to back him up. He had to resist the impulse to touch his ear. Fin had insisted they swing by his flat on the way out here. He'd grabbed a small microphone and an ear-piece receiver he'd 'borrowed' from the tech division and never returned.

"It's so I can stand a stall or two down from you but still hear what you're saying," he'd explained. Emily had dressed in a cashmere sweater and overcoat. Fin hadn't bothered to ask if she carried a weapon—he couldn't imagine her going to such a thing without one. He just assumed the heavy coat hid what he hoped would be a large gun tucked somewhere she could easily access it.

And so now they were at the part he hated most—the waiting. Emily stood outside a small craft table, sipping a steaming takeaway cup of tea. He was two stalls down, trying on a variety of hats and scarves and using the mirror to continually check behind him. One of the joys of having his looks and colorful outfits was people expected him to be excessively vain. No one would think twice at him continually checking himself out in the mirror. It wouldn't cross their mind that he might be checking their tail and assessing others who lingered a bit too long or showed undue interest in either himself or Emily.

It was a perfect cover.

Time seemed to crawl by. Fin marveled at how Emily genuinely didn't seem like she waited at all. She sipped her tea and appeared patient enough as if she could stand there until midnight. Fin had to resist the temptation to check his watch every fifteen seconds. His inner antennae quivered as a tall man in a knee-length black coat paused a few paces behind Emily. Something about the way he coolly assessed her, his gaze roaming and simultaneously dismissing her, captured Fin's attention.

Discreetly, Fin pulled out his phone. He tapped the pad of a finger onto the camera app, turned so he could see the man clearly in the mirror, and snapped a photo of him. Zooming in from a full-body shot to just his face, Fin waited until the man looked up — checking his surroundings — and gave Fin a perfect head shot.

Darkly tanned, the man was exotically foreign. With shoulder length brown hair, thick eyebrows and eyes so dark they appeared almost black, he looked as if he should be wearing a loin cloth and playing Tarzan somewhere, not dressed in an impeccable suit and long, woolen Burberry coat.

"Emily," the man said. Both Fin and Emily jolted at the sudden noise. Fin assumed Emily was taken by surprise because she hadn't seen the man behind her, but Fin was shocked how well the transmitter worked. The man's voice in his ear sounded as if he stood right next to him.

"James, sorry, my mind was wandering." Emily held out a hand and they shook. Fin wondered if it was all an act on her behalf — if she'd actually been aware of him all this time. He couldn't imagine her letting her mind stray at a time like this.

"I've brought those documents," James continued. "But I admit I became curious on my way over here. You've always insisted on retaining the right to decline any job, you won't even accept a non-refundable deposit up front like most of your competitors. Why the meeting?"

"You're quite persuasive. You seem determined to follow this through. I also feel you're correct, you have earned my trust. You deserve the right to prove your point and convince me."

"You've never indicated that as an option before," James insisted. "And you've never struck me as a woman who lets herself be convinced of anything."

Fin frowned and forced himself to select a different hat and try it on. His instincts knotted his stomach. Something really wasn't right here. Why wasn't James showing her the so-called evidence? Why was he questioning Emily like this? Was he merely suspicious, or was there some deeper game being played here?

"You asked me to trust you, and that's what I'm doing," Emily said dismissively. "I'm perfectly happy not to take the job, but you insisted, so here I am. We can leave it right here if you prefer."

"Oh no, my dear," James replied smoothly. Something in his tone had Fin turning around. He could sense something...but he had no idea what. Everything inside him said the whole deal was going south, but he couldn't put a finger on what. It was like the feeling he'd had mere seconds before something disastrous occurred, that devastating knowledge he was missing something and not being able to spot it.

James reached inside his jacket and alarm shot through Fin like a bolt of electricity. James' large body angled into Emily, the breadth of his shoulders protecting his hand from anyone's view.

In Fin's earpiece he heard the muffled *wisp* of a silenced bullet.

Emily gasped.

Her knees crumpled.

Fin's heart stopped beating.

Dimly, he was aware of James walking on as if he'd merely exchanged a few pleasantries with a stranger and they were done. But Fin only had eyes for Emily.

She sank to her knees on the dirty ground.

She clenched her hand to her breasts, right above her heart.

Fin could all too easily imagine her holding in the pumping blood, the pain she must be feeling. An ache unlike anything he'd experienced rammed into his chest. For a moment he couldn't breathe, couldn't think. He wondered if he was suffering a heart attack.

He raced to Emily as she crouched forward, clearly struggling to breathe, her shoulders and back shaking with the effort dragging air into her lungs caused her.

The thought she might be dying galvanized him. He couldn't have jolted to attention faster had someone jabbed him with a cattle prod.

"*Help!*" he screamed at the top of his lungs. "Somebody help me. Please!"

Taking one last look, Fin realized those few seconds of frozen shock had cost him any chance of following and catching James. Writing him off instantly, Fin sank to his knees in front of Emily, clasped her shoulders and lifted her so he could assess the damage.

People leaned over them both, asking in a confusing cacophony of voices and noises what was wrong and what did they need.

Emily labored for breath. Fin pulled her hand away, shocked there was no blood.

He ran a hand over her chest, finding the bullet hole exactly where he expected it, between her breasts and directly over her heart. There was a singed tear in the soft cashmere of her sweater, proving his ears hadn't deceived him. She had been shot. Sticking a finger through the small hole, he then pushed against a hard plate.

She wore an armored vest.

"Oh, thank fuck for that," he panted, sagging with the intensity of his relief. Emily grimaced in his arms, still struggling to draw breath. Her face flushed darkly and it seemed to take everything she had just to wheeze in a few pants.

"...hurts..." she barely managed to squeeze out.

He huffed a laugh, swung her into his arms and stood in a smooth motion. "I'm sure it does. I'm also sure you're going to have the mother of all bruises marring that beautiful skin of yours for weeks to come. I'm taking you to the hospital."

"Vest," she puffed, still winded and clearly in pain.

"I can see you're wearing a vest, a fact for which I am eternally grateful. Undoubtedly you'd be dead if not for that."

"Didn't realize it would hurt so much," she groaned. Fin kissed her forehead and carried her to the car. Her color was returning to normal and she still struggled to catch her breath, but he could see now that she was fine.

"No one could possibly explain how great the pain is," he agreed. "I'm tempted to spank you though.

What if he'd gone for a head shot? Or your neck? A vest only covers your heart."

"He's arrogant." Emily wobbled as he put her on her feet so he could open the car door for her. "He also knew he'd need time to escape. A heart shot is quick, silent and gives him time to leave before people would have noticed I'd fallen."

Fin helped her into the seat, buckled her in and came around to the driver's side.

"Heart shots can be fatal," he agreed, smiling at her. She'd certainly shot him directly through the heart, her aim perfect. He couldn't imagine his life without her. Starting the car, he took her hand in his, pressed his foot to the accelerator and peeled away.

"They're not that bad." Emily grinned back at him, seeming to think along similar lines to herself. "Yours was shocking, but it hit me dead center."

"And your aim is always true," he agreed.

They linked their fingers together and he drove them to the hospital. He knew she'd be fine, but would feel better once she had been checked over and cleared by a professional.

"James is still out there," she said.

He nodded. "I know. We'll get him."

Showing more than words could express her trust in him, Emily relaxed back into the seat next to him and rested her head on his shoulder. She sighed happily and closed her eyes.

"Yeah," she agreed. "We will."

KNIGHT TAKES QUEEN

Chapter One

"Oh. Well aren't you a sneaky little bastard?" Jane Harvey muttered to her computer screen as her fingers flew over the keyboard. Clacking filled the air of her tiny office. Leaning closer to her monitor, Jane moved her eyes as code scrolled past rapidly.

"Oh yeah, didn't expect that, did you, you jerk?"

As one of the technology experts for the Agency, Jane enjoyed regularly pitching her talent against all sorts of twisted new systems. This one, however, took her by surprise at just how ingenious it was. Even as she watched, she saw the hacker mutate the code she'd inserted.

"Hmm, that's new," she murmured.

"Talking to your screen again, Jane?"

Jane turned for a moment and saw Peter leaning casually against her doorframe. Even as her cheeks flushed warmly, she forced her attention back to her computer. Though how she was to ignore how tall and well built he was she didn't know. Peter was far too handsome — Jane had been crushing on the blond, blue-eyed man for months now. In pinstriped suit pants with a matching charcoal vest and blue shirt, Peter should have looked old-fashioned or stodgy but somehow he managed to look sexy.

"Sometimes it's the only one who understands half of what I say," Jane replied lightly as she continued to try and thwart her opponent's attempts at slipping a Trojan into the Agency's secure network. "I know I haven't made the next move on our chess game. I'm sorry. I thought you were on leave. Isn't Maria due to pop any day now?"

"No worries, I just wanted to duck in and see you. It doesn't always have to be about our little game. But yes, I'm hoping they reassign a new partner to me before she gives birth. I'm a lot harder to fob off if I'm present rather than hassling on email or something," Peter said.

Their online chess game—a thoroughly against the rules one to boot—had started out as a bit of a lark. Peter had been bored and roaming around. He'd noticed her playing a game by herself. That had been the first proper, non-mission related conversation they'd had. One thing had led to another and when she'd narrowly beaten him he'd immediately challenged her to a rematch.

That had been a few months ago and their friendship had blossomed with a healthy dose of competitiveness, too.

Peter came into her office and his large presence filled it immediately. He took the only other chair and sat next to her. Jane forced herself not to fidget. Even with her eyes firmly locked on the screen, she couldn't help but be electrically aware of how close he was. She smelled the light, masculine scent of his aftershave and reminded herself she was in the middle of something. There wasn't time to turn, stare, and drool over Peter Abrams right now.

"Heaven forbid you grow bored, Peter," Jane teased him. "No wonder you never made it as a tech. It's often days of humdrum banality then something like this pops up. I swear this time management has gone a bit far. I know we need to be tested, to be proactive in upgrading our systems. But really…"

"What have you found?" Peter leaned in closer and Jane caught her breath. He glanced at her and once more she found her face heating.

"Well." She cleared her throat. "I'd only be guessing, but my money is on that new technician, Roger, flexing his muscles. I'm well used to everyone else's bag of tricks and this isn't something I've come across before. The coding is amazing and convoluted. Well finessed. The target is trying to insert a Trojan into our system and I'm fighting him off, corrupting his code in real time."

"How do you know it's Roger?" Peter asked as he peered at the screen with her.

Jane smiled. "Well, it has to be someone from in the unit. They were already inside our firewalls and safety systems when they tripped a flag and came to my attention. Every couple of months management tests us like this, sets us against each other to playact duking it out. It keeps us sharp and can be used as a tool to make sure we understand how to follow the Agency's procedures and fail-safes even when under pressure. It's an exercise for us, like your physical tests or training courses."

"But how can you be sure it's not just a very good hacker?" Peter pressed. "Don't these exercises usually come with prior notice?"

"Well," Jane paused, distracted. "Well yeah, usually. We're never told the date or anything. But a general notice that sometime in the coming month...but, but this can't be a real attack. They started inside the system."

She heard herself repeating the last comment like a talisman. Jane stopped typing and looked directly at Peter for the first time that afternoon. Her insides froze as panic threatened. Peter's cool blue gaze didn't waver from her and for the first time since she'd met him Jane didn't have the urge to run her hands through his thick, blond hair.

Jane spent a vital moment mentally casting back over her recent emails.

Peter was right. There hadn't been a warning that system checks would take place anytime soon. And while a part of her still believed this was just an internal exercise, she couldn't take that risk.

Jane turned back to her monitor with strengthened purpose. She hadn't cut any corners earlier, but this time she started double saving everything and using remote locations to back up data. It hadn't entered her head that this might be a 'real' threat. And while the Agency's countermeasures were good, she wasn't going to take any chances.

"I need you to get into the bottom drawer of my filing cabinet," she said to Peter without shifting her focus from her work. "There should be a box with an external hard drive in it. It's about the size and weight of an old VHS tape."

Jane heard Peter open the drawer. A minute later he sat back down and held the hard drive out to her. She nodded her chin to the desk.

"Plug it into the power board and connect the USB into my desktop, please," she said. Dropping her flirtatious manner, she sat forward on her chair. This was pure work and she was focused. "Once I start saving some screenshots and dumping the code he's shedding onto the external I can maybe distract the hacker and try to back trace him."

"Shouldn't there be some sort of alarm you're meant to activate?" Peter asked as he followed her instructions.

"Sure," she replied. Jane's gaze remained glued to her monitor. She touch typed and only occasionally glanced at the jumble of letters to be sure she didn't make a mistake. A single incorrect keystroke right now could prove disastrous, but unfortunately time was of the essence. As fast as she worked though, her opponent was equally swift. But Jane was no novice and despite the sweat she could feel trickling down her back, she didn't miss a step.

"The problem is that whoever this is, they've gone to great lengths to appear as if they started inside the system. Which was sheer brilliance on their part." Jane couldn't help but admire the sneakiness of whoever this was. She fervently hoped it was the cocky new technician, Roger. She'd even admit to his face he'd had her scared. That was far better than the alternative—someone on the outside who had managed to hack in.

That thought made her knees wobble.

"If this really is an attack on us," Jane continued, "and they're good enough to get in without tripping any of our catches, then they've certainly got the talent to be aware when I sound the alarm. Anyone who knows our system this well will be alerted when I activate our documented countermeasures. I'm hoping to get enough data quickly so I can use it later to track the source, after I've locked us down."

"And how long is 'quickly'?" Peter asked.

Jane risked a brief look at him. His gaze was intense and focused on the screen, but under her stare he glanced at her. She smiled. Jane mightn't be the most confident of women around, but when it came to matters inside a computer, she knew she was queen.

"Faster than you could believe possible." She flirted, but quickly grew serious again. "Besides, once I lock the system down all hell will break loose. No one will be able to work, not the hacker and not us either. It's never been used in real life before, only in drills, so I want to leave that until the last second necessary."

Jane focused once more fully on the task she'd set herself and Peter fell silent. The only sound in her cramped room was typing and the odd muttered curse.

The world narrowed until only Jane and her nemesis existed. Code flashed before her and she mumbled as she tried to hack back to find the source. Time stretched on, though microsecond-long glances at the clock on her screen showed only three minutes had passed since Peter had walked into her office.

"Son of a bitch," she whispered. Jane had an inkling of what the hacker's true purpose was. It made her equal parts angry and afraid.

"What?" Peter insisted. "Jane, explain it to me, your screen seems full of gibberish and symbols. I'm not fluent in…code, or whatever that is."

"I think we're in deep trouble," she replied, though her focus wasn't on the handsome man next to her, but on what felt like the dark opening into the abyss beyond.

"Have you got what you need?"

"No," she replied. Lightning fast, she keyed in more strokes, and seconds later flickered her glance down to make sure the external hard drive had finished saving the data she'd logged with it. As soon as the light went off, indicating the device had finished, Jane snapped her eyes back to the screen.

"Unplug the hard drive and remove the USB connection," she said, haste making her sound curt even to her own ears. "I'm fairly sure locking the system down won't make us lose more than a few minutes' worth of data, but after all this effort I'd hate to have it crash and lose what little I have simply because we were lazy."

Peter followed her orders immediately in quick, economical movements. Jane saved a few more tendrils of code from the hacker to the memory stick she'd been using earlier—back when she'd thought this was just a routine drill—and kept part of her attention focused on Peter and his progress.

When he had the backup safely disconnected from everything she took a deep breath and mentally fortified herself.

Each technician had trained rigorously for this moment, yet she'd hoped never to do it. Even in training it had made her stomach clench uncertainly. She pushed the thought that this might be a hacking or terrorist attack out of her mind. Hopefully this was just a surprise test, one she'd pass. Jane had no idea if she should do something as drastic as issue an immediate lockdown, she wasn't even positive she had the authority to do so.

But if this *was* real—or even meant to simulate a real scenario—Jane knew she couldn't hesitate.

She typed a long series of letters, numbers and symbols. After the first six characters the rest of the string was hidden by asterisks on the screen—one of many safeguards.

"Jane, it's taking too long to track this person. You need to initiate our countermeasures now," Peter urged her.

She wasn't surprised that he couldn't differentiate this code with any of the others she'd been typing in the last ten minutes. No one outside of the high level managers and the techs like her knew this sequence.

What most people didn't realize was even if she stopped typing now, the system would still go into lockdown, but in a far different, more difficult to undo format. Yet another fail-safe, in case an analyst was being forced to act or was under threat of death.

Sometimes her job, safe as it might appear against the other agents who fought for their country, scared Jane silly.

"Jane—" Peter said as the entire power grid shut down.

Lights went off. Phones stopped ringing, computers, faxes, everything connected to the power winked out in the blink of an eye.

In the unnatural silence, Jane realized even the air conditioner had stopped humming, something she didn't think she'd ever been conscious of in the first place.

There was a minute of absolute, complete stillness then a cacophony of noise as people reacted. Shouting sounded all around them as other workers raised their voices. Orders were given and many calls were made simultaneously. Items clattered and there was the sound of moving furniture—and more than a few bangs and swear words uttered as other workers stumbled into things. All throughout their floor, carefully controlled pandemonium ensued.

Jane had no doubt the other floors under the Agency's aegis held similar well-contained pandemonium.

She lifted her hands from the keyboard and swallowed hard, her mouth completely dry. Jane turned to look at Peter. Her office was half dark, as many of them were now. Even though it was midafternoon, Jane didn't have a window and without the florescent lights there was very little natural light to be had.

"I'm guessing you dropped by because you were bored?" she said in an attempt to be lighthearted. It fell a bit flat, but at least she'd tried.

"Darling, you're one of the most complex, interesting people I know," Peter said in his mildly flirtatious way. "And now I know neither of us are going to be bored. Come on, let's go face the music."

"This was on me," she insisted. "Not you. Once my legs stop shaking I'll track down old Bones and try to explain what I think was going on."

"Jane, you don't have to do this alone," Peter said in an astonishingly soft tone. "I'm a witness to you doing everything conceivable to protect our system. And I urged you to lock it down. That doesn't rest entirely on your shoulders. Besides, I think we should take this to Preston, not Bones."

Jane frowned, not sure she'd heard him right. Feeling drained, she rubbed her hand over her face in an attempt to make certain this wasn't some twisted dream.

"Bones is head of IT," she reminded him. "I work for him, and this was an IT matter. Lockdown procedure can't possibly fall under anything else. Why would we take this to your boss, to a field manager?"

"You thought this was an internal hack attempt, right?" Peter asked.

She nodded. "I'm still not convinced it's not some weird new test process they're keeping secret. Why?"

"Think about it," Peter urged. "If we have a mole, or a traitor, should we really inform one of the people capable of being behind it?"

"Bones might be a bit old-fashioned, but he's a patriot. He takes his duty to heart. No way is he behind this," Jane scoffed.

Peter stood and held out his hand to her. Jane took a slow breath and lifted her gaze to meet his.

"Trust me, darling," Peter said with conviction. "Let's at least take this initially to Preston. He might agree with you and call Bones immediately. But I'd rather keep the intel you gathered and what few clues you might have quiet for now. Do you trust me?"

Jane licked her lips and thought hard. She trusted Peter. They'd only been friends for a few months, ever since she'd been promoted to a senior technical level. When she'd moved out of the pool area where most of the analysts worked and into this tiny, wonderful office, he'd started swinging by more and more frequently. She'd known Peter Abrams' reputation for years though.

He was a solid man, unquestionably honorable. He might have a disarming smile, a cocky attitude and a nonlinear thinking brain, but she'd never had cause to doubt his integrity.

She wasn't going to start now.

Jane reached out and took his hand. He helped her stand. She pulled the memory stick out of her desktop and dropped it into the pocket of her skinny jeans. With her free hand she collected the external hard drive and looked around the small room, feeling faintly lost.

"This is either the biggest case I've ever worked, or I'm about to be demoted back into the group pool and people will be cursing me for months about lost reports and data files," she said half to herself.

"I told you I'm never bored with you, darling," Peter said. "You wait and see, this is going to be fun."

She couldn't see his smile, but it was in his tone. "Sure," she agreed half-heartedly. "Fun."

Chapter Two

Peter couldn't help but admire Jane's resilience. She'd clearly shown nerves a few times, but overall the lady had plenty of guts. Exactly as he'd come to realize lately.

He'd relished watching her privately for a moment earlier, leaning against the doorframe and just admiring her. For months now he'd been lusting after her from afar. She looked relaxed and stunning in her tall boots, navy skinny jeans and a flowing, airy silk shirt. Long brown hair fell in wavy curls half way down her back. Big, dark eyes had been focused on the screen and a partial smile had tilted the corner of her mouth up. Her creamy, pale skin had nearly glowed as she'd typed furiously against her supposed colleague.

Even when she'd appeared to admit it might be an outside force hacking them, Jane had not wavered. She'd become more determined, her inner strength had shone through, right until the reality of the situation seemed to crystallize — until she'd needed to pull the plug on the entire Agency's system.

It was a serious enough breach that even Peter hadn't been as blasé as he'd tried to appear. They really might be in some serious trouble. But the alternative, letting someone hack them, was unthinkable.

Jane showed no desire to remove her hand from his. Their fingers remained twined together as they walked to Preston's office. Subdued chatter filled the large communal area. People stood in clumps talking amongst themselves, a few agents seemed determined to reboot their computers, swearing about lost reports. Mostly, however, everyone seemed more curious than genuinely alarmed.

Peter did notice, however, that Jane kept her gaze averted from her colleagues and they skirted away from having to pass the other technicians in the group area. He had a feeling everyone would soon enough know who was responsible. He was determined by then they'd have enough evidence that there wouldn't be blame, only praise at Jane's quick thinking and dexterous fingers.

They hurried down a hall and as they came close to Preston's office, the large man strode through the doorway and halted when he saw Peter and Jane heading his way.

Preston Jones had worked his way up from a field agent to manager. Peter held the man in high esteem. Preston was tall, physically fit and still in shape despite his decade or more out of the field. Dark skinned and with a sprinkling of salt in his hair, Preston had never forgotten the flexibility needed when out on assignment.

Peter appreciated having a boss who understood that, sometimes, rules couldn't be followed when snap judgments needed to be made. Peter might strain against some of the enforced rules and regulations, but he'd never had cause to be more than mildly irritated with Preston. They got along well.

Jane halted as they came up to Preston and swallowed once more. Peter grinned at his boss, who sighed.

"I should have known," Preston said with more resignation than annoyance. "You two had better come in."

Peter caught Jane casting him a quick glance. He smiled at her and squeezed her hand gently. Without a word, he let her go and waited for Jane to step into Preston's office first. He followed her and closed the door behind them.

Preston had a small window and there was plenty of ambient light for them to see. The room was silent though, the lack of electric hum noticeable.

"I take it you both know something about what's just happened?" Preston started.

Peter noticed Jane sit forward on her chair and as she opened those luscious, pink lips she seemed to try and order her words. Peter hurried in and beat her to it.

"We were being hacked," he said calmly. "From the inside."

Preston frowned. "If it came from within the Agency, are you sure we were being hacked? Couldn't it have been routine...I don't know...maintenance or something?"

Peter and Jane exchanged a glance. This time, he let her answer.

"I'll be honest, at first that's exactly what I thought." Jane threaded her fingers together in a nervous manner. "There are a number of layers of security that anyone hacking in from the outside should have needed to bypass. Within those layers there are many, many flags that should have been raised to warn us someone was attempting to breach the system. Nothing like that had been tripped."

"So what makes you think this wasn't one of your co-workers doing a drill?" Preston asked.

Jane frowned and shrugged. Peter tried to not notice how this action made the loose, flowing silk shirt she wore slip a little over her shoulder, baring the pale, delicate skin for a moment before the material slid back into place.

"A few things," Jane continued, having no idea of the distraction Peter found her to be. "There wasn't a warning that a drill was forthcoming. Peter reminded me of that. To date, we've always been given a heads up when one was in the works. Also, a colleague wouldn't have let this go as deep as it did. I've never, ever felt like our security was threatened enough to even contemplate initiating a lockdown. That's a last-ditch effort. A drill or training shouldn't have pushed us that far. And this hacker was good. They weren't flouncing around, waiting to be noticed. They were focused, direct and very talented. If I didn't work here, if I hadn't been instrumental in helping set up a number of these security fail-safes, I'm not sure I have the talent to make it in, especially not unnoticed."

"So this person is good? Or had help from inside the Agency?" Preston suggested.

Jane nodded. "Possibly both. Plus, there was one last thing that tipped me over the edge. If this had been a drill, there are rules we follow, areas where we don't delve. Even for training purposes, our confidential files are off limits. Eyes only and all that. This person was sifting through a section of those. Looking for something specific, from what I could gather. When I realized that, I knew I had to shut us down."

"Is that why you said we were in trouble?" Peter said, recalling her words earlier.

"Yes. I already half believed this was a hacker, someone from outside. When I understood they were searching our files, possibly even downloading our records, I knew it wasn't one of us," she insisted.

Peter stared at her, and Jane found herself blushing slightly under that intense blue gaze. "At first I thought it was a joke, or maybe a prank. When I realized how serious it was, I didn't want to speak of it, even in the office. I know I can be paranoid, but I was thinking like the hacker, deep in the coding. If I'd mentioned how serious it was someone might have been listening nearby, or maybe walk past my door at just the wrong moment. By keeping my worries and thoughts to myself, by not giving them voice, it couldn't come back onto me. Does that make sense?"

Peter nodded. The tension she'd seen in his face had eased. She smiled gently at him. "I trust you, but coders by nature are a security-conscious lot. Paranoid."

For some reason she couldn't fathom that this seemed to amuse Peter. He grinned widely. Jane turned back to Preston and tried to collect her thoughts.

"Techs love to push the envelope and we all want to, uh, go where we're not necessarily invited. But I can't believe anyone who works here would blatantly abuse their power like this. The repercussions of it, of being caught, are too great. The risk isn't worth the reward, or I certainly don't believe it is."

"But an agent could, wittingly or not, have helped this person," Peter pointed out.

Jane didn't seem to like the thought. She pursed those lovely lips together, but she didn't contradict him, either.

"Do you know what files this person was after?" Preston asked. He rested his elbows on the desk and steepled his fingers together. Tilting his head down, he tapped his index finger on his nose a few times. Peter knew the deeply thoughtful look well.

"I've saved what I could from our exchange," Jane said with hesitation.

When she glanced at Peter he smiled warmly at her and nodded encouragement. Jane lifted the deceptively bland looking black box, the external hard drive they'd used. "I was too busy trying to fight the Trojan the hacker was using as a distraction to really pay attention. Once it became clear it was our secure archives that were his real target I pulled the plug as quickly as I dared."

"What's on our archives? Sorry, our secure archives? Is there a difference?" Preston asked.

"Everything we do is secure to one level or another," Jane explained. "But the secure network is supposedly invisible to anyone on the outside. Unhackable."

"Could that be why this person entered the system somehow from the inside?" Peter asked. It made sense to him, but he certainly wasn't a specialist in that area.

"None of this is supposed to be possible," Jane said, then sighed. "I'm half tempted to track the person down just to ask them how they managed it. I'll be disappointed if someone within the Agency helped them. I'd much rather think there's some genius out there smart enough to crack our system. We could learn from them."

Turn a hacker onto our side? Peter mused.

Recruiting shifty people wasn't common within the Agency, and Peter had a feeling it wouldn't be the easiest thing to do. Someone who got a thrill from hacking secure systems wasn't the sort of rule-following, team player that was required to make an agency like theirs work. Still, he could see where Jane was coming from.

With the online world still blossoming at a huge rate, they needed every advantage possible. The rules were constantly shifting, and what was unthinkable a year—or even a few months—ago was suddenly necessary. It was something to at least keep in mind.

Peter exchanged a look with Preston.

"Do you know what they were after?" Preston asked again.

"Oh, sorry, no. But I'm fairly sure they didn't get it," Jane reassured them. "The hacker was still going strong, seeming to sift through the files. They were the old case files. Hmm, stored in section covering all the missions from ten to fifteen years ago. I'd need to check, once the system is up and running again, but I believe everything is there. Old projects and cases. Information drop points, old classifications and personnel files. Everything."

"In the secure network? Really? From that long ago?" Peter asked, a little surprised.

This time it was Preston who nodded and replied. "Codes and exchange procedures can resurface in the damnedest of places, even decades later. Just think, if you've retired and moved on, but perhaps stumble across something twenty years down the track, wouldn't you revert to old procedures you knew would catch our attention to hand the data over?"

Peter could see Preston's point.

"And all personnel files are always kept heavily encrypted and under the strongest security possible," Jane added. "Partly for deniability once an agent retires, but also for their own safety. But after seven years we bundle together certain times, for the inactive work at least. And that's where our hacker was searching."

The lights flickered and came back on. The faint whirl of the air conditioning filled the room. Peter glanced at Jane, who seemed relieved. Preston checked his phone, lifting the handset and replacing it.

"Still dead," he said. He pulled his BlackBerry out and winced. "We need to decide what we're going to do. Soon. The phones will be next and there's only so long I can stay dark."

Peter studied Jane carefully. He'd flirted mildly with her for months now, their chess games a form of careful foreplay as they each sounded the other out. He'd come in today specifically to see her and hopefully ask her to dinner, or something. Earlier this morning the upcoming few weeks had been filled with endless possibility. No partner. No casework. No imminent danger or possibility of having to pick up a go bag and leave at a minute's notice.

He'd thought a few weeks of getting to know Jane better, possibly even starting something serious, was a small slice of heaven. He should have known better. Life was never boring around the Agency.

But this time it was slightly different. It wouldn't be him leaving her behind, or needing to keep things secret. They could work together. Hell, she'd said herself she was tempted to track down this hacker.

No way did Peter want her doing that alone. Unprotected.

His stomach lurched just at the thought of it.

Peter turned in his seat to face Jane. He hoped he wouldn't need to convince her, but was ready with everything in his arsenal if called for.

"I think Jane and I should go on a bit of a fact-finding mission," Peter started, keeping his tone light and easy. "There's no use anyone getting worked up until we understand exactly what data Jane's managed to collect."

"But the system is down," Jane replied with a small furrow of her brow. "And Bones will have rounded everyone up by now. They might even know it was me who initiated the lockdown. That's no secret. I used my code to do so. I'm not ashamed of my actions. It will be clear once they get into the network that it was me. There's paperwork for me to fill out and I bet I'll have to write a report, or more than one."

"Don't you want to know who was behind this?" Peter cracked open the door, hoping Jane's innate curiosity would lead her through willingly.

She shifted on her seat to study him. "Well. Yes."

"And don't you think Bones will keep you snowed under with a million reports, checks and boring things until he has all the analysts on the case?" Peter added.

Jane made a face. "Probably. I don't see where you're going with this. The system is *down*. Locked down. Remember?"

Peter cast a quick glance at Preston. The man nodded — a short gesture to indicate his approval.

"Well, we can log in remotely can't we?" Peter said in his most reasonable tone. He threw in a charming grin to help sweeten the deal. "Why don't we go somewhere, an Internet café or your place, or anywhere with Wi-Fi, if you can use your BlackBerry. You can get in and analyze the data you saved on the hard drive. We can see if you can track the hacker then get onto them before they have a chance to lose their nerve and escape..."

Peter let the image settle for Jane. Preston leaned forward in his chair.

"Peter is an excellent agent, as I'm sure you're aware," Preston said. "All we need from you is the information you can give. Instead of working at your desk like usual Jane, you'll be out in the field. You can get a taste of how the other half live, following your own leads, unearthing the clues and working the case."

"A field agent?" she said, dark brown eyes wide. "But, but I'm not rated. There's training, the exam. Physical tests. I'd never pass any of them, not that we have time or that Bones would allow me."

"You wouldn't be an official field agent," Preston replied. "But you'd certainly be acting like one, and I'd support you both fully. Peter will be your partner and help keep you safe. If there's even a hint there might be danger, you're to call it in and we'll get backup to you both immediately."

Peter didn't miss the very stern, hard look Preston shot at him. Peter had no question that this was completely nonnegotiable.

"I certainly can't make you," Preston cajoled. "But at this moment I believe you're the only person in a position to help us. You have the talent, you know the background and I believe you have the desire to find this hacker. Is that right?"

Jane smiled. "Well. Yes."

Peter caught Jane's eyes and they stared at each other a moment. The air seemed filled with a dozen questions between them, all unvoiced and silently answered.

Jane nodded.

"We'd better get moving," she suggested. "Can you explain to Bones what's happened? Please? And smooth things over with him? I really do love my work. I don't want him angry with me or a black mark to appear on my record."

"Leave it to me," Preston said as he stood.

Jane and Peter both followed. Jane blinked, as if she was waking suddenly from a dream. He didn't want to press her, but he needed to know their next step. And that was in her hands, not his.

"Where are we heading?" Peter asked gently.

Jane turned to him. He waited while she thought. "My place," she said after a short pause. "I've got some equipment there. Things that will help me work this out. It doesn't feel right though. Surely as a field agent we should be out there asking questions?"

"One move at a time," Peter assured her. "Think of it like our chess games. We can plot and plan a few steps ahead, but right now we need to focus on the next part, then read the board once we see the other moves."

Jane nodded. "Then my place. And we can go from there."

Peter shook hands with Preston and touched his fingertips to Jane's elbow, gently escorting her out into the hallway. Even though the lights had come back on, people milled about, talking eagerly with each other.

"Let's take the stairs," he murmured close to her ear. "We're not in trouble, but I'd rather not get dragged in to make explanations right now either."

He nodded to a few friends as they greeted him, but both he and Jane kept walking with a purpose and no one stopped them.

"One second," she said and ducked out of his grasp.

Peter was about to protest, but watched as she slipped around a few groups of co-workers who still hung around. Almost immediately he understood. Her office was only a few meters away. Jane walked in and less than a minute later came out with her bag. The hard drive was no longer in her hand, but the purse bulged suggestively.

Jane returned to him and they continued on their way.

Jane's mind whirled. So much had happened in an incredibly short time. What felt like only an hour earlier, she'd been happy at her desk, routine tasks flowing through her terminal while she flirted lightly with Peter. Now she and the fellow agent were jogging down the stairwell headed for the car park, on a mission together, of all things.

"I caught the tube in, I'm close to the station," Jane suggested, not wanting to put Peter out too much.

"I'll drive us to your place," Peter said. "We can decide to leave my car on your street later, but I'd like to have the option of our own transport in case we need it down the track."

Jane nodded and was about to speak, but suddenly her skin started crawling. Her instincts screamed at her. Someone was watching them. She glanced around and for the first time realized how isolated the parking garage was.

Thick concrete pillars created dozens of blind spots. Crappy fluorescent lighting did little in the dim area. Sounds echoed and made it impossible to judge distances. Was that faint scraping noise just behind her, or on the other side of the space?

Jane hadn't received much field training. As an analyst, the vast majority of her work was based at her desk, behind her computer monitor. That was where she shone. But it didn't mean she wasn't aware of her surroundings, or that she wasn't interested in an adventure out in the real world. But the feeling was awful and scary. She'd never experienced this creeping sensation, as if there were eyes that bored into her, monitoring her every move.

She shivered. It felt like ants crawling over her skin and down her spine.

Peter stopped and turned back to her. Jane hadn't even noticed she'd frozen in place. He tilted his head and small creases appeared at the edge of his eyes as he focused on her.

"Someone's watching us," she whispered. "Can you feel it?"

Peter smiled but she could see it was a fake one. He glanced around and held out a hand to her.

"Where?" he asked. A tight knot eased in her stomach. His tone was light, curious, but she could tell from his protective stance that he believed her. His glance around might've appeared outwardly casual but she knew he was scouring for clues.

He trusted her instincts.

Warmth seeped into her, helping to keep the ebbing panic at bay.

Jane tried to probe her subconscious. Why was she so certain they were being watched? Where could they be hiding?

"I can't tell," she started, her tone still soft. "You know when someone's watching you, not just idly glancing, but focusing on you? I've got that icky skin-crawling sensation."

"Are they nearby?" Peter asked. "Can you feel a direction from the gaze?"

Jane quickened her breath as she started to feel light-headed from the stress. She needed more oxygen in her lungs and brain. Until now she'd never understood how anyone could have plenty of knowledge—book learning—but real life be something completely different. She felt woefully underprepared.

Reaching out she then grasped Peter's offered hand. Courage returned with the strength of his grip.

"I'm okay," she said, more for herself than anything else. "Let's have a quick look around."

They wandered around the garage. Jane wanted to twitch and jump at every shadow, but she forced herself to remain calm, to look carefully behind every post. Strangely, the deeper they moved into the darker areas, the less certain she felt anyone was there. It was only as Peter led her back into the middle of the walkway, into the light and normal thoroughfare, that she felt her paranoia rise again.

"There's no one here," she insisted, completely puzzled. "How does that make any sense? I can *feel* someone watching, I know it sounds crazy but we're not alone. I only sense it out here, in the middle of the light, on the proper pedestrian pathway. But there's no one here, look."

She turned around, and as far as she could see not another person was in view. So why did she feel as if she were being studied, watched, tracked?

It was completely illogical. Maybe she was losing it? Falling into the paranoid world of double and triple crosses.

"I don't know what to say," Peter replied gently. "Let's get into the car and talk about it on our way."

Despite his sweet words, Jane felt her face flush hotly. There wasn't an ounce of condescension in his tone, but she felt silly. Jumping at shadows and imagining boogey men where there were none.

As they crossed to the car, she again felt that sensation.

Jane whipped around, glancing everywhere. She scanned the area intently. She *knew* she wasn't imagining it. Squatting, she checked under the cars, then slowly rising she lifted her gaze to the ceiling and around all the corners she could see.

Finally, her eyes rested on one of the many security cameras.

Her paranoia flared, but common sense finally kicked in.

"We're dealing with a hacker," she said. Peter nodded but remained silent, following her gaze and not seeming to understand.

"Hackers break into databases," she tried to explain. "We're not a physical, gung ho breed. Or not normally. We sit back, we creep in, we analyze the data and steal what we can. The first thought of most hackers wouldn't be to jump into action and chase around their person of interest. They'd sit back, study, follow remotely."

She nodded her chin to the security camera then calmly turned her back to it and focused on Peter.

"Think about it. Security cameras are everywhere. They're normal. I don't even notice them anymore really. Practically every other corner in London has a small camera, CCTV, security. We must walk past thousands of them every day."

"They don't ping on our personal radar," Peter caught on. He flicked his gaze to the camera then quickly away again. "We're so used to them everywhere we don't pay attention to them anymore."

"What if the hacker *is* watching us, but not here. Through that." She silently indicated the cameras around them. "It's not like you need to physically follow someone anymore. And to be honest, I bet anyone with this skill set wouldn't think of it first, or be confident enough. But hacking into a security system, that's easy. Following us through the cameras, that's totally in their comfort limit."

"Well I'm not too worried about that," Peter replied.

Jane shook her head.

"Don't be so sure," she warned him. "Sooner or later watching us remotely won't be enough. I have no idea what this person wants, but we need to find out. Quickly."

"But you said they'd be happy just to watch us. So let them stalk us that way. Who cares?"

"Sooner or later it won't be enough," Jane insisted. "If they can watch us, while we stumble around trying to get information on them, they'll end up knowing far too much while we're still in the dark. And if they really have such a strong purpose, monitoring us from afar will only work for so long. The need to confront us will grow. They'll need to force us to give them whatever it is they want."

Peter looked thoughtful. He seemed to finally understand where she was heading.

"I don't know about you," she said lightly. "But I don't want to be around when whomever is on the end of that camera finally gets up the courage to confront us. They've got skill and a whole lot of righteous purpose. They might be hanging back for now, but that won't last forever."

"We need to know what they want," Peter agreed.

"Absolutely. And we need to sort it out," she insisted. "Before their patience runs out. I don't want to meet them face-to-face without all the answers."

"We'd better get moving." He led her at a fast pace through the underground parking garage. Neither of them looked at the cameras. Jane struggled not to glance up at them constantly. She'd never before noticed how they were *everywhere*. Thankfully, Peter soon beeped open his car. Jane touched his jaw with the tips of her fingers as he held the door open for her.

"Have you really thought of everything?" she asked him.

Peter turned to her, and Jane needed to catch her breath. He could be cocky, but she knew he had plenty of experience. His confidence was well-earned. Peter grinned at her. She tried to remain calm as she slid into the seat. Leaning close, he winked cheekily at her.

"I'm always a few moves ahead of you, darling. You should know that by now," he said lightly, picking up their flirting right where they'd left off.

She chuckled and shook her head. "Like Queen to K4?"

He laughed and bent to kiss her cheek. She flushed. The kiss had been spontaneous, sure, but it was hot and came so easily, so naturally. Her heart pattered hard, responding to his sexy move. Heat zinged through her body.

"You surprise me far more often than you should," he complimented her.

Grinning, Jane decided to remain silent. A smile was all she needed to give him. Peter closed the door and went around to the driver's side. He slid into the seat and started the engine.

"The game might have to wait a little bit," he finally said as they pulled out of the garage and into the heavy London traffic. "Right now we have a hacker to trace. Much as your charms and beauty are pulling on my every attention, I can't become too distracted until we have our own next few moves plotted."

"And after we know what the plan is?" she asked, sounding curious.

Peter grinned widely. "Why then the field is open to us both. It's your move, darling."

Chapter Three

Jane pulled out her keys as they walked to her front door. She desperately tried to remember how clean her place was. She vaguely recalled doing her breakfast dishes before leaving that morning and Jane was fairly sure she didn't have any dirty clothes lying around. But she thought she might have left the coffee table in a bit of a state and there was a good chance her rubbish needed to be taken out too.

She sighed to herself as she opened the door and took a quick peek inside.

When there was nothing jumping out at her screaming embarrassment, she moved to the side to let Peter enter.

"I usually tidy up more thoroughly on the weekends," she apologized. "Let me clear the table off and we can get to work. Would you like some tea? I could probably rustle us up a sandwich too if you're hungry."

"Tea would be great, thanks," Peter said.

Jane tried to ignore the curious, interested manner with which he surveyed the room. Once more she cast her glance around, noting the furniture was only slightly threadbare. Books and texts crammed her shelves and there were a number of piles semi-neatly stacked up. The few prints she had on the walls were colorful and made her happy.

It wouldn't kill her to run a vacuum over the floor, but neither was the place dirty or dusty. Nothing to be ashamed of.

Dropping her bag on the coffee table, it only took her a few minutes to then quickly pick up the half dozen books scattered about. She opened her personal laptop and booted it up then picked up the mug she'd had her morning tea in. Putting the items out of the way, she then switched on the kettle.

"Take a seat anywhere, I'll hook everything up in a minute and we can get started," she offered. "You should be prepared though, it might take me a while to get this all sorted."

"Really?" Peter replied, looking surprised. "That long?"

Jane smiled wryly.

"I know you guys think we techs are miracle workers, but you'd be amazed how much work actually goes into the stuff we do for you all that time," she explained. "This won't be as easy as tracking down a GPS signal or hacking a target's phone records."

The kettle boiled and Jane set out a tray. She placed two mugs, teaspoons, a small jug of milk and her sugar bowl neatly together. Jane filled her favorite teapot—a ceramic one with little gadgets painted onto it, laptops, mobile phones, remotes and such—and let the tea steep a minute. Satisfied, she carried the tray and placed it on the coffee table.

"Okay." She sat on the couch and typed the password to unlock her laptop with a quick motion. The long sequence flowed smoothly and she didn't need to check the keyboard as she started to immerse herself in the work she'd set up.

Peter sat beside her and the warmth from his body distracted her for a moment.

She recalled her manners.

After reaching out she stirred the pot then lifted the lid and checked the tea was dark enough for her taste. Happy with the color, she looked at Peter as she poured him a mug.

"Milk? Sugar? I don't have any lemon, I'm afraid. I take mine strong and black," she explained.

He shook his head. A single curl fell forward on his brow. It was difficult to resist the impulse to brush it aside.

"Just a touch of milk, please," he answered.

The smile he sent her was a killer one, one of his most charming. Not only did Jane blush, but she felt her body heat all over. *This could get complicated.* She tried to convince herself the importance of focusing on work and not how devastatingly handsome she found the man next to her.

Jane handed him his tea then poured herself one too. A quick blow then a hasty sip, Jane winced as she nearly burned her mouth on the steaming brew. She returned the mug to the table and opened her bag. Pulling the hard drive out, she suddenly recalled the memory stick in her jeans pocket.

She dipped a hand to retrieve that too, then plugged everything in and started to open tabs on her screen.

"So what did you manage to find?" Peter asked, peering at her screen intently as he drank his tea.

While she found it easier to focus when his entire attention was on the computer and not her, Jane still found herself unnaturally aware of the close press of Peter's body. His warmth. His scent. She blinked. After taking a deep breath she forced her mind into action.

"Hopefully I've got everything leading up to the shut down," she started. "I'll spend a little while pulling apart the coding of the Trojan. Hackers have a tendency to leave signatures and if I can find one that should help us work out who was behind this. I also want to try and narrow down where the hacker was trying to look, and download files. That mightn't be as telling, it's possible they were just grabbing anything as proof they were present."

"But they went to an awful lot of effort to get in, right?" Peter asked.

Jane nodded. "Absolutely. We have every safeguard possible, and you know the lengths we go to stay on top of technology. Security is everything in our business. I hate to admit it, but it's a strong possibility someone might have helped our stranger in a back door somewhere."

"Does anyone stand out to you?" Peter asked.

Jane pressed her lips together and started separating out the code for the Trojan. After a minute or so, she hoped Peter would let it drop. She wasn't that lucky.

"Jane? If you know something—"

"I don't," she insisted. "But...well, Roger has been trying to prove his balls to anyone who'd be willing to pay attention. But that's standard for a geek when they start a new job. Everyone begins at the bottom, and tech geeks in particular don't like the blow to their ego. By and large, the only way to earn your way up is to prove you're as good as you insist you are. And that takes time. Roger's young. He's impatient."

"If you think he might be involved you need to say something. To Preston or perhaps Bones."

"The only reason I mentioned Roger is because he's new," Jane insisted. "I don't know him like I know everyone else. There's no way anyone could help a hacker get in from the outside. I mean, seriously. Can you imagine George, or Tiff spouting off secrets like that? Forget the treason, ignore the fact it'd ruin their careers, something they're passionate about. But a geek doesn't share their secrets, not when it comes to coding or their trade. Everyone has their own little tweaks, their personal twists and flashy signatures. You'd need to torture one of us to get that information."

Peter sat back on the couch and linked his hands over his flat stomach. Jane glanced at him, but he seemed lost in thought. Figuring she'd given him something to chew over, she returned to sifting through the reams of data. Usually Jane hated analyzing code, especially stuff she hadn't written. A double space where there shouldn't be one, a comma instead of a period, everything had consequences and it was a painstaking job.

"You really don't think anyone inside the Agency leaked something?" Peter said after a few minutes.

Jane shook her head. "Not knowingly. I'd also be surprised if anyone's private computers had been hacked and the information gleaned that way, but this guy—or girl—is good. Scary good. It wouldn't have taken much. If anyone had got sloppy, or say let their lover check emails on their laptop after work, something like that. You'd be amazed how one tiny mistake could open doors to someone this talented."

Losing herself in the code, it took her a minute to realize Peter had fallen silent. When that thought registered, she felt the weight of his gaze upon her. Blood thrumming again, she cast a quick glance behind her. Peter watched her steadily, those beautiful blue eyes of his seeming to study every inch of her.

"What?" she asked. Jane lifted a hand to her face, wondering if she had tea around her mouth or something.

"If you were going to hack in, how would you do it?" Peter asked.

"I know the system inside out," Jane reminded him. "So that's not really a fair question. I know where the small holes are that we can't do anything about. And I know how the security has been layered. It'd be like testing a ten year old on their ABCs. Once you know something from every direction, it's easy to spot the ways to break in."

"Still, indulge me," Peter insisted. "How?"

"Well," Jane shrugged. "There would be dozens of ways, but I'm fairly creative when it comes to hacking. I like taking the road less traveled, so to speak. The first way that comes to mind is I'd hack into your account through our chess matches. I bet you don't encrypt your keystrokes when you're playing a game or Skyping with your family. It's natural to use every level of security for work or email, that's common sense. But if you're just popping on to see if I've made a move in our game, my money would be on you'd not bother to use the security for work. Once I was in your system it's a short, tricky but possible step into the Agency's."

"That's it?" Peter asked, dumbfounded.

"Yes, but how many people know you play chess with me at all hours of the night?" Jane pointed out. "And on your work laptop no less."

"You'd not try to get in on my—or someone's—BlackBerry?"

"No way," Jane shook her head. "Far too much security on those. We know how easily hacked they are, so we fortify them as much as possible. And everyone knows not to do anything truly sensitive on an open network like that. Again, I know the system, so I know exactly where our weak spots are. Unless we're talking an ex-Agent with a vendetta, I doubt anyone could possibly know the holes. It's our job to make sure as little vulnerability as possible is present. And we're damn good at our work."

Peter stretched out on the couch. He crossed his legs at the ankles, linked his fingers and laid his head back on the cushions, staring at the ceiling. Jane had never seen him think so deeply, but left him to it. She sipped her tea and typed.

Immersed in the code, she forgot for a few minutes that Peter was even there. She cheered when she found a recurring signature in the guts of the Trojan.

"You beauty!" she crowed, pleased with herself.

When Peter sat up in a single fluid motion her heart pounded. She recalled his presence again. "What did you find?" he asked.

"The bastard used a really tricky encryption package," she groused. "Otherwise I'd have found this much sooner. I think I found their tag."

"Tag?"

"Their signature, or screen name," she explained. "Look here, here and over here. TruthSeeker. Tags can be really hard to spot sometimes, because they're proper words, sometimes even a part of the code itself, but the fact it's such a recurring name makes me think it's the hacker's signature."

"Interesting, that says a lot about this person," Peter said.

Jane agreed. "I wouldn't expect a hacker to be as obtuse as to choose a tag like AngryFuckYouGovernment. Only novices or dabblers use something like that. Forget the millions of red flags such a name would raise, but who'd share information with someone like that? But TruthSeeker doesn't sound like some disenchanted youth or a wannabe terrorist. It sounds like someone on a mission of their own."

"And a person who wants answers," Peter added. "This isn't someone trying to bring the Agency down, or destroy the government. This person is looking for information, trying to uncover a secret very important to them."

"Well it could be someone wanting to expose corruption," Jane added. "I know we're clean, the Agency I mean. But it could be a person who thinks we're a cog in a big machine they don't trust and want to expose. TruthSeeker might mean something different to this hacker than it would to you or me."

"We definitely need more information," Peter added. "Could TruthSeeker be part of his password? Or a key to unlock the decryption you mentioned?"

Jane shook her head. "A hacker this savvy, this talented wouldn't make such a rookie mistake. But now I know the decryption they're using, I can set to unlocking it. That will just take time."

"Can we trace them?"

"Not until I've unlocked everything," Jane said. "Back-tracing to the source is the last step here. Besides, the more I learn about this guys' style, the easier it will be to recognize them if I see their work again. And who knows, there might be hints. Coding is a very personal thing—it's like writing or speech. I can pick up traces of where they've learnt tricks, perhaps even a mentor. It's like a language analysis, learning where they grew up, what kind of school they attended. We've only scratched the surface."

"So it could be a while?"

"We're not talking days," Jane shrugged. "It's the decryption that will slow us down. Why? You have somewhere else to be? I can handle this alone if you need to go."

"No, that's not what I meant." Peter chuckled. "I've just been thinking about what you said earlier. How if you were going to break in you'd piggyback on me, on our game. What if the hacker does know someone at the Agency?"

Jane remained silent while she thought about that. She didn't like the connotation, but had to admit Peter had a point. This hacker was smart, incredibly so. And they had to be determined to have got so far inside the guts of the Agency's system. Jane just hated the thought someone she worked with, someone she knew and trusted, could be a party to this. Knowingly or not.

"I don't know how we could even start to cut that list down," she finally said. "It wouldn't have to be a tech, it could be anyone. All agents use the system, for emails, data checking, reporting. Access could have been taken from anyone."

"Maybe just keep your eyes open for a name, or even a code name or number that recurs," Peter added. "It could be a link back to someone in the Agency, something we could use."

"Okay," she replied. Jane sighed, feeling a bit down. The thought of having a traitor made her feel depressed.

"What's your code name?" Peter asked.

Jane frowned, needing a moment to change the direction of her thoughts. "What? Why?"

"I've never seen you use one, and the way you spoke earlier, how it's a part of the hacker's identity, a part of them, it made me curious. What's yours?"

Jane blushed a little, somewhat embarrassed. "ForestQueen."

"ForestQueen?" Peter repeated. "Oh you can't leave me hanging like that. Explain."

"Originally it was the name I'd use in gaming circles." She pretended to focus on her laptop. She continued to type as she talked. "Mum and Dad would take my brother and I camping as kids. I loved the forest. Just being something small in the wilderness, trees enormous and towering over me. I felt free, like I could breathe. Sometimes I found the city so stifling, especially school. When I was a teenager, my dad taught me to play chess, and the name took on a deeper meaning. It stuck. I like it."

Jane jumped a little as she felt Peter's touch. He rested his warm hands on her shoulders. She tensed, but as he gently massaged her she relaxed again. He rubbed a particularly tight knot under her scapula and Jane had to bite down on her lip to not moan.

Damn, his hands feel good.

She fluttered her eyes shut and relished the intimate rubbing. A lot of the tension she'd been feeling since discovering the hacker melted away. Jane deepened her breathing and let her anxiety go.

"Isn't that just a little better?" Peter whispered in her ear. He continued to knead her shoulders and back.

Jane thought she'd died and gone to heaven.

"What would you use as a code name?" the question popped out of her mouth before she could stop it. The words were out there, so she decided to go with it. "You just use Peter_A online, which is cheating really. So if you needed to pick one, what would you use?"

"I'm not sure," Peter answered, though she could hear the thought in his tone. "Knight, maybe?"

Jane let her imagination soar. A few naughty suggestions popped into her mind — SexyKnight, FuckMeKnight, HardKnight. She didn't voice any of them.

"ShiningKnight," she said after a moment. "It needs to be tailored to you, the name. You're not just any knight. You routinely try and save the world, make our country a better place. Corny as it sounds, that's who you are and what you do. So. ShiningKnight."

"That sounds better," Peter admitted.

Jane leaned her head back and turned slightly. Peter had that devastating grin, the charming, sexy one that made her pussy clench. He leaned in closer and paused for just a second. Jane drew in a breath, certain he was going to kiss her, but not wanting to move in case she was completely losing her mind.

Peter must have seen something in her gaze, he bent his head and pressed their lips together. Her heart pounded. Jane tilted her chin up and pressed her mouth harder against his. When Peter opened his lips she followed him. Flicking her tongue out, she then met his and they clashed intimately together.

Someone moaned, though Jane was too lost to have a clue who it was.

Nothing else mattered. The world could burn around her and she wouldn't care. Only this moment, Peter and those delicious lips of his held her attention.

Chapter Four

Jane's nipples tightened, the lace of her bra rasping against the tender skin. She shifted her legs, her labia already slick with need. "Peter," she murmured. He moved his hands lower, tracing a pattern down her back until he palmed her hips. His motion caressed the silk of her shirt against her already sensitized body. It felt exquisite.

"I've wanted you for weeks," he panted. "Months."

"What took you so long?" she pouted. "If I'd been any more forward I'd have had to strip naked and do a dance around your desk."

"Now that would have been a sight," he chuckled.

"How about I give you an eyeful now?" she teased. After saving her work—an automatic gesture, Jane knelt on the couch. She straddled Peter's hips and sat in his lap, facing him.

Peter lifted his hands and ducked them under her shirt. When he stroked the tips of his fingers against her stomach, she clenched the muscles tightly in response. Electric pulses shot through her, his touch alone enough to make her body quiver.

"Wow, that's something I've been missing," she said, breathless.

"Why don't I give you a hand?" he offered.

His voice was deep and thick. Jane pressed a palm against his crotch, pleased to find him already hard. Peter tugged her shirt up and over her head. Jane raised her arms to help him. Her pretty, lacy pink bra looked sexy and Jane was glad she usually wore nice underwear, even on a regular day.

"You know, I've wanted to do this for ages," she said in a low tone. One by one, slowly and enjoying the experience, she unbuttoned his vest. The material was clearly part of his three-piece suit, the same dark shade and with matching pin stripes as his pants.

"Where's your jacket?" she asked, curious but still riveted to the removal of his vest.

"Probably still slung over the back of my chair," he replied. "I didn't think to grab it. We needed to leave in a bit of a hurry."

"Well I love your vests," she said. "They make you look debonair. Almost anyone else would look stuffy in them, or old-fashioned. But you have this cheeky little smile, a cocky tilt to your chin and your eyes make me melt. Somehow you just look dead sexy and it drives me wild."

"I had no plans to change my wardrobe," he replied, "but you can be sure nothing short of a natural disaster will make me alter it now. That's the best compliment I think I've ever got."

Jane pulled his vest off and started in on his crisp shirt. Peter strung a long trail of kisses down her neck and over her breast. It made her usually dexterous fingers fumble. The circuits in her brain fried.

"I love how you're just a palette of color," he murmured against her breast. He swiped his tongue out, licking her though the lace of her bra, causing her to shiver. "Even here, in your flat, there's brightness everywhere. In the cushions, your throw rug. You're bright and happy all the time, even when you complain about a new system or how many cases you have to cover over the weekend. You're like a glorious rainbow."

Jane had just pulled Peter's arms free of the shirt when he finished his last comment and paused, not quite certain if his words were a compliment or not.

"A rainbow?" she repeated.

Peter shrugged. "I have no blood in my brain — give me a bit of leeway. It's bright, colorful and pretty."

Jane laughed. Peter bent forward and kissed her. His lips were so soft she moaned. Hungrily, she tasted him and again they parried their tongues. Only as one of her boots fell off her feet did she realize he had unzipped it and had gone to work on her other.

Eager now, she struggled a little removing his trousers. When Peter canted his hips up so she could pull his pants and briefs down his legs, his cock sprang free. Jane stood and quickly finished undressing. Her gaze was riveted on his delicious dick, long, thick and pale. She licked her lips, eager to taste him.

She lifted her gaze and caught his glance. He grinned at her, that charming, cocky smile she was falling in love with.

Naked, she knelt between his legs. Jane reached out and cupped his sac in one hand, closing her fingers around the root of his shaft with her other. She leaned in to him and opened her mouth. When Jane swallowed down around him, Peter groaned and she looked up. He'd thrown his head back, pressed into the cushions of the couch. His blond hair was becoming mussed, a few curls falling free now.

Jane wished she had a free hand to run through them, as she'd wanted to for ages. Instead, she bobbed her head and sucked down hard around his cock. Salty pre-cum wept from his slit and she lapped it up. Gently she rolled his sac between her fingers and lifted her hand, stroking his length in time with the movement of her mouth.

"Fuck, that's amazing," Peter cried out. He reached and threaded his fingers through her hair. She hummed as he pulled her further down his shaft. Jane felt full to bursting with his possession, but loved the sensation. Peter thrust his butt up, pressing deeper.

Jane swallowed, knowing her throat constricting around his length would add to the sensation. Peter moaned. She wanted to smile. Driving this man incoherent had been a fantasy of hers for a while now. She quickened her motions, working them both higher. Only as she felt his balls tighten and his erection begin to pulse under her tongue did she stop.

"I want to feel you inside me," she panted. Jane stood though her legs were shaky. Her bedroom felt a million miles away.

"Condom. Wallet," Peter groaned.

"Fantastic," she said, unable to articulate further. Jane crouched and dug a hand into Peter's trousers on the floor. She pulled out his wallet and extracted the condom. After sheathing him, she climbed back onto the couch.

"Are you wet?" he murmured.

Jane spread her legs and let him feel for himself. Peter reached out a hand and swept his fingers along her slit. The action both parted her lips and collected some of her cream.

"Damn," he panted.

Jane shivered as he repeated the motion several times, lubing his cock and nudging her desire higher. When he finally pressed a thumb over her clit she lifted up on her knees, keening with pleasure.

"Now," she pleaded, unable to bear waiting a moment longer.

Peter's warm hands clasped her waist and helped her settle astride him once more. Jane angled his cock and slid onto him in a long, slow, blissful motion. He stretched her thin walls and Jane had to gasp as she struggled to fit him entirely inside her. She clenched her inner muscles, contracted them, then released.

She was exquisitely full.

"Ride me, darling," Peter gasped. "Fuck yourself on me."

The rude words had her blood heating and Jane took her pleasure. She lifted herself up and sank back down, slowly at first. All too soon her channel relaxed and need had her growing wetter. Jane stared at Peter as she moved over him. He'd widened his eyes and his face had become flushed.

Just as she'd longed to do, she ran her fingers through his thick hair. It was silky, soft and curled around her fingers as she drew his mouth up to hers. Kissing him passionately, she watched him watch her. The intensity of his gaze, his unwavering interest in her both bolstered her confidence and made her feel simultaneously shy.

Never had any lover stared so deliciously at her, as if he needed to memorize her every move, every pant and gasp. Had she any doubt previously about his interest in her, this would have banished it. Peter seemed entranced, desperate to sear this coupling in his brain.

She felt cherished.

Faster and faster she brought their bodies together. Skin slapped against muscle. The sounds and scents of sex filled the air. Jane clung tighter to Peter. When he winced she moved her hands to his shoulders, giving herself a better grip as she rode him hard. Jane tilted forward and cried out as her clit rubbed against his body.

"Nearly there," she gasped.

Despite her earnest desire to watch every moment, she closed her eyes to try to hold onto her control just a few moments longer. Warmth closed around her breasts and she had to see once more. Peter had latched his mouth around her nipple. He sucked her hard and this drove her wild. She shattered, lost herself in the pleasure.

Her orgasm ripped through her body. Jane moved, though it felt clunky as she struggled to make her limbs work correctly. Peter placed his hands on her shoulders and drew her down. Jane bent and cried out again as he thrust hard up into her, filling her deeper. Her clit grazed over his muscled belly again and she felt electric sparks shudder through her.

Peter groaned and she felt his body twitch, shake and finally fall still.

Panting and sweating, Jane collapsed against him. They sank into the cushions. Replete, satisfied, she closed her eyes again and enjoyed the sense of his warm body beneath her, his masculine scent enveloping her.

* * * *

"Knight takes Queen," he murmured in her ear.

Jane stirred, with no clue if seconds or minutes had passed.

"Hmm?" she blinked and sat up.

Peter grinned at her, that naughty, cheeky smile charming her once again. "You heard me," he said.

Jane bent down and kissed him slowly, thoroughly. She pressed her lips against his, then flicked her tongue out to taste his.

"I would have said Queen takes Knight," she parried, feeling proud. "Maybe you can take me next time."

Jane carefully climbed off the couch. She paused just for a second to take a mental picture of Peter there. Mussed and rumpled, his hair curly and wild-looking. His eyes were large and just a little glazed, his body hard, muscled perfection, his cock lying dormant but still impressive against his thigh.

"Bathroom is the third door down the hall here," she said. "I'll just be a second then it's all yours."

"You've got a delicious arse," Peter called out as she walked out of the room. "I want a bite of if next time."

"Maybe if you ask nicely," she said back.

Jane closed the bathroom door behind her and spent a minute freshening up. She left a clean washcloth on the basin for Peter and made sure the small waste bin was in clear view next to the sink.

As she returned to the living room she recalled the search they were in the middle of. Jane doubted anything had popped up yet, but she felt eager to return to it. One thing she could say about sex with Peter, not only was it amazing, but it gave her a massive boost in endorphins. She was raring to get back to work with him.

"All yours," she said when she came into the room.

Peter had already got up and was standing by the window. She had a good view out onto the street. Curious, she came up beside him and peered out. She didn't see anything very special out there, but then it was the same view she'd seen every day for a few years now. Jane pressed a soft kiss to his cheek. Peter smiled and for the first time she noticed tiny crinkles at the edge of his lips. She thought they were adorable.

"All well out there?" she said, half teasing.

"Nothing too suspicious," he said.

Jane had to press her lips together. She thought Peter was taking this whole protection thing a little too seriously, but then she wasn't field rated and had never been in any danger. Who was she to judge?

Just as she turned to go back to her laptop, Peter cupped her jaw and drew her to face him again. She glanced at his eyes and for all his handsome smiles and lighthearted manner, his gaze was serious.

"You shouldn't be nervous, but I also don't want you to be blasé," he cautioned her. "Someone out there, a stranger who is smart enough and determined enough to crack the Agency's security, is looking for something. They're not fooling around, so I don't want you ditching me or running off on your own. We don't need to be paranoid, but I need you to take this seriously."

Jane hadn't felt this was a game, but she had forgotten how frightened she'd been earlier when it had dawned on her this was real. This wasn't some test, or her co-workers pulling a prank or matching wits in a friendly tussle. Peter was right. There was someone out there and they were serious. Prepared, dedicated and smart.

She nodded.

"I've waited all this time for you to make a move," she said lightly as she lifted a hand to brush through his mussed curls. "I'm not going to waste this chance and ditch you. You're stuck with me. I promise."

"I'll take that for now," Peter replied, a little cryptically.

She wasn't completely sure what he meant, but her mind had turned back to the virus. He kissed her chastely. Jane reached around and patted his naked arse. The man had buttocks of steel. She understood the appeal of wanting to take a bite out of them.

Restraining herself, Jane walked back to the pile of clothes strewn over and around the coffee table. Peter collected his things and headed toward the bathroom. Jane picked up her pink lacy knickers and stepped into them. A tap on her keyboard had the screen coming out of the power save mode and a blinking window caught her attention.

Forgetting that she was practically naked, she sat on the couch and typed quickly.

After her discussion with Peter, his insistence that someone had to be in collusion with the hacker had stuck. She just couldn't let the thought go. So she'd set up a remote search, looking for unusual activity, like password changes that weren't requested by the system or long dormant files that had suddenly been opened.

Jane widened her search parameters to include email accounts and archived files that had been recently accessed and weren't connected with open cases. While she waited for the search to complete she stood and pulled on her underwear, jeans and socks. After slipping her shirt over her head, she sat down with renewed energy.

Jane opened the hard drive and backed up the memory stick she'd managed to save. She started to search for what files, exactly, the hacker had been trying to download.

"Any luck?" Peter asked as he returned, fully dressed, into the room.

Jane glanced at him then smiled. While he had his vest on, it remained unbuttoned. It gave him a somewhat rumpled look that she had to admit made him even sexier in her eyes. She was a little sad to see his hair combed back into its usual neatness once more.

"You're edible when your hair loosens enough to let your curls free." The words came without conscious thought. Jane made a face but had to admit it was the truth. He did appear luscious when his hair was unkempt.

"Those damn curls are the bane of my existence," Peter sighed. "My mother insists that even in a blue sailor outfit and wearing a tie I was mistaken for a little girl until I was almost two years old. No one could imagine a baby with a head full of golden curls could possibly be a boy. Besides, your hair is curly, you know what a nightmare it is trying to keep it tamed."

Jane had to give him that point—it could be a pain controlling her hair. But something about it just made him irresistible to her.

"I'm seeking abnormalities in our system," she said. "I've not found anything so far, but I have a few avenues to look down before we get desperate."

"How about I refresh the tea, then?" Peter offered.

Jane cast him a grateful glance as he put everything back on the tray. She heard him enter the kitchen and the click as he turned the kettle on.

She tried to not think about how right and natural he looked inside her kitchen, and focus on the small matter of finding the traitorous hacker who had breached what should have been one of the most secure networks in all of England.

Chapter Five

"You'd be amazed just how many files have been accessed in the last four weeks." Jane sighed as she scrolled through the large list her search had resulted in. "We must be crazy, this is worse than looking for a needle in a haystack."

"You said the hacker was searching through the archives, maybe try to reduce the list to archived files only," Peter said.

Jane lifted an eyebrow at him. "This isn't my first day on the job," she pointed out, keeping her tone teasing. "This list is archived files. It would be ten times as big if active cases were included. There's what, three or four hundred agents, not to mention consultants, government officials and assorted others who have more limited access to our files. The list I collated was focusing on the archived data."

"Okay." She noticed Peter seemed to stumble mentally only for a second before readdressing the issue. "Talk to me about the hacker and the path they took then. Walk me through it from the start. I'll try and look at it with fresh eyes and maybe if I ask the right question it might tip something off for you."

Jane turned her attention back to the screen and brought up a new window. Peter's idea was smart. Maybe if she set out a brief timeline they could learn something from the trail the hacker had left. Thank goodness she'd saved everything possible from their interaction.

"The first flag was brought to my attention a little after three this afternoon," she started. "Someone had bypassed a first level password request on our Middle East files. This is a new baby of ours, we have a pop-up that appears every now and then that says your password has timed out and to re-enter it to continue."

"I've come across those," Peter pointed out. "They're bloody annoying. Are you saying that's intentional on your part?"

"Absolutely," Jane replied as she continued to type. "If someone has piggybacked onto an account, or like this guy somehow managed to hack in, it's quite possible they don't know the official password at all. We're actually testing this system out right now. Camouflaged as just a routine spot check, and very easy to slither out of for a talented hacker, it's innocuous enough to not raise awareness. But it sends a red flag to us. Think about it, Peter. You might find it annoying when you're in the middle of doing research for a report, but you just grumble, type in your password and *voilà*, you're back on track. But for someone who doesn't know the right answer they just shrug and sidestep it with a bit of fancy typing. They think nothing more of it because it's so easy, but we get a red flag saying someone's not typed in the correct response."

"Pretty sneaky," Peter said, though there was admiration in his tone.

"You have no idea." Jane chuckled. "Some of the stuff we do...well, it'd blow your mind, I'm sure."

"No doubt," he agreed. "So you got a ping that someone had evaded a routine check."

"Exactly. I went to look into it and they'd very cleverly spoofed their log in details." Jane noticed Peter seemed a little blank at this. She explained. "When you log in, all sorts of details are in the code. Like which computer you're using, your ISP location, dozens of things. This guy had made it look fuzzy, so a simple, quick check couldn't identify it. It's simple and very accurate. It's why I thought someone in IT might be fiddling around, looking to see who was on the ball and able to catch them. A test."

"Okay, so what were they looking for?" Peter asked.

"That's the problem I've been facing," she replied. "And where this guy's true genius started to shine through. They weren't a kid in a candy store, rushing up to the toffee they wanted immediately. They browsed and muddied the waters. The virus they tried to plant didn't help either."

"Virus?"

"The Trojan, I thought I mentioned that," she said. Jane sighed and swiveled to look at Peter. "Once I started following the hacker, tagging the files they opened and trying to guess their real purpose, I noticed they'd left flags of their own. Like little bombs. And if more than a few were set off the code would join together and the markings made it clear it would act as a virus and start cloning our system."

"You're starting to lose me," Peter shook his head.

Jane pursed her lips together and tried to summarize a bunch of technical stuff. She didn't want to bore Peter, but he needed to understand.

"This is just my gut feeling, I have no proof to back me up yet," she insisted.

He nodded and she continued, "I think the hacker was using the files they tagged with the virus as a sort of alarm clock for themselves. Once a certain number of files were opened and the virus started to piece together it would act as a signal for the hacker that they needed to go. Ingenious, I wish it was something I'd thought of. It also means anyone—like me for instance—who stumbled upon it would immediately start trying to deactivate the virus. It's just in our nature. As soon as we see code that will ruin our system we want to get rid of it."

"A red herring," Peter said thoughtfully.

"Well, sort of." Jane smiled wryly. "It was real, that damn virus would have crippled our system. Think of it more as insurance. Any technician worth their salt would have ignored what the hacker was actually doing and immediately gone to neutralize the virus."

"That I can understand," Peter agreed. "So you were trying to unravel the code of the Trojan and not continue following the hacker. Which is why we don't know what they were really after."

"Almost, but not quite," Jane said with pride. "I'm a woman. I can multitask. Yes, my main focus was on the Trojan, but I also kept tabs on the hacker and what they were searching for. That's why I have a list of the files they opened. I'm just not sure how helpful it will be. Clearly the hacker had enough brains to open a bunch of random files as well as the one they were interested in. It was only as they started to download files that I really started to panic and hit the shut-down switch."

"Well what were the files they tried to download?" Peter asked with a bit of snap in his tone.

Jane held up her hands. "Calm down. I'm not stupid, that was the first thing I looked into. And I don't think they'll help. Just like the hacker tagged dozens of seemingly random files, they also didn't rush in and start downloading something that makes any sense. It was some of our standard operating procedures. The information packet we give out to applicants looking to take on a courier job, the standard nondisclosure form everyone signs and a few of our leaflets we hand out at careers fairs and seminars."

"What? Is that all?" Peter looked completely puzzled.

She felt a bit proud having stumped him again. "At the time I had no idea what the hacker was downloading, I just knew they were accessing and saving files from the inner guts of our system. I was already worked up, paranoid and on edge. The simple fact they were taking *anything* was enough for me to flip the switch. But as I said, I'm not a dummy. The first thing I did was try and work out what those files were, I just think they might be a dead end and I jumped the gun a little."

"Could this be some weird sort of job application?" Peter asked. "Maybe a way to get our attention and prove how good they are?"

"Eh." Jane wrinkled her nose. "Can you really see Bones wanting to hire someone because they hacked into our system? It's an incredible risk for them to take if what you're saying is true. And that virus wasn't a joke."

"Okay." Peter rubbed a hand over his face in what looked like a tired motion. "So we've got quite a bit of information but none of it looks relevant or helpful."

Jane shrugged. "It might make sense when we have more pieces," she said hopefully. "And we do have the name from the code. TruthSeeker."

"Is there anything unusual in any of those files they looked into?" Peter asked.

Jane stared at him. "You're kidding right? Can you honestly think of a single mission you've been on, or any case that you've ever heard talked about where something didn't seem strange, or go wrong, or need explaining to an outside person? Our work is inherently oblique and full of missed or wrong turns."

"True. Well, stranger than normal," Peter amended.

Jane turned back to the laptop and started typing. "How about I do a data mining chart?" she offered. "See if there's anything that links these cases."

"That sounds good."

"It might backfire," she warned. "With such a large number of cases there's bound to be a bunch of flotsam. Similar agents on the peripheral, managers in charge of the cases, I'm worried this might set us off on the wrong path. The hacker went into the archives, so it has to be something old or closed they were after. Otherwise why bother?"

"This whole exercise might be moot," Peter pointed out. "Hackers don't need a reason. Hell, this could all be about some twelve-year-old pimpled little boy trying to prove his balls to his mates, being able to hack into a secure government facility just because he has the talent and can."

Jane shook her head. She finished setting up the search, sent a silent prayer upwards it would yield *something* they could use and sat back on the couch.

"This guy was too organized for that," she insisted. "This took planning, patience and guts. I know anything is possible, especially in our industry, but I'll be astonished if this turns out to be some kid on a lark. The hacker came prepared with the virus, knew what they were looking for and was intelligent enough to muddy the waters of their path. This wasn't a joyride done on the spur of the moment. There was intent behind their breaking into our system."

"Which begs the question again, how did they get into our system?" Peter asked.

"I wish I knew," Jane murmured. "That might give us more clues as to what they were after and who they are."

"Hey," Peter said softly. "You're doing an awesome job. Hitting brick walls and finding your way out of dead ends is part of the work. Flying on gut instincts and really tenuous links is something we all do every day."

"I guess I'm just used to things being a bit more clear cut," she admitted. "I'll get a call, or a memo, and be told 'get information about nuclear waste in Brussels', or who knows what. I'll put an enormous folder together full of innuendo, hard facts, Internet rumors and anything else I can lay my fingers on and send it off, then move onto the next request. It's different, seeing the whole case and trying to muddle through."

Peter cupped her jaw then ran his thumb over her lower lip. Jane's heart fluttered. He scooted closer to her and their thighs pressed together on the couch. Peter was so close she could hear him breathe. When he grinned at her, crinkles almost formed a dimple in his chin. His blue eyes were hot and focused so intently on her they warmed her blood. She lifted a hand and ran it through his soft, recently brushed hair.

"You must charm all the ladies right out of their knickers," she murmured. "That grin of yours should be classified as a lethal weapon, not to mention your gaze, your hair."

"Don't forget my body," he teased roguishly. "I'm quite the package."

"And modest, to boot," she laughed.

"There's only one lady who I want out of her knickers," he lowered his tone and whispered. "You."

Jane lifted her head and met his hard, pressing kiss. Peter leaned forward and they lay on the couch, she on her back, him settled on top of her. Jane tightened her hands on his scalp, his hair brushing over her fingers silkily. Peter undid her jeans and tugged them down. Jane wriggled her arse and helped him pull them down her thighs. Her lacy underwear soon followed, crushed against the denim as he bared her to the cool air.

"I swore to myself I'd wait, do this right the next time," he groaned. "But I can't help myself now. I wanted these long, slender legs of yours wrapped around my shoulders, your delicious pussy open fully to me."

"We can move to the bedroom," she panted. "There's time while the computer searches, we don't have to wait here."

"Condoms?" he asked.

Jane blinked her eyes and swore.

"I haven't been..." she swallowed, not wanting to admit how very long it'd been since she'd entertained a man sexually in her flat. "I'm not prepared properly, no. Sorry."

"Not such a bad thing," he flashed that wicked smile again. "I only had the one myself. I live in hope, but it's been a while for me, too. I guess that means I need to be creative."

"Creative?" she squeaked when he shifted lower and bent his head.

He swiped his hot, wet tongue over her labia and he grazed his teeth over her clit. Heat blossomed and the world of possibilities unfolded before her.

"Peter," she couldn't even finish her thought, let alone form a coherent sentence. Three fingers slid inside her, stretching her passage. Jane arched her hips up, desperately seeking more friction as her pulse skyrocketed. He pumped his hand and air rushed out of her lungs.

"Oh yes," she cried out.

Peter used the thumb of his other hand to stimulate her clit, he fucked her at a hard, steady pace with his digits and Jane found herself worked up in minutes. He strung small, nipping kisses across her belly.

"Lick me again," she panted. Jane tilted her head and watched him. Without shifting his gaze from hers, he lowered his head to her crotch, grinned at her in that same, charmingly wicked manner and licked her pussy with deliberate slowness. He lapped at her slick juices and finger-fucked her deliciously.

Words failed her. She could only watch and hunger for him.

"I can feel you tightening around me," he murmured. "Your channel's like a vise. I wish it wasn't my fingers, but my cock. I want to slam inside you, pound you and fill your every orifice. I want to watch you fly so high and be there to catch you when you fall."

"Holy shit," she gasped, his words turning her on as much as his actions.

"Come for me," he urged.

Jane could feel her climax building. She started thrusting her hips, fucking herself down on his fingers and increasing his tempo.

Her computer beeped. They both looked at it but didn't stop.

"Do we need to —?" Peter asked.

Jane reached out and snapped the lid closed on the device.

"Bollocks to them. Don't stop," she insisted.

He didn't question her.

The interruption had taken her back a notch, but Peter rose to the occasion. He lowered his head again and focused on her clit. The wetness of his tongue lubed her and his hot breath had her shivering in delight. The rough friction drove her higher and all too soon she was crying out, needing to come.

Mouth buried in her pussy, Peter couldn't speak anymore. He thrust his fingers inside her and she felt a gentle probing at her anus. Jane pressed her feet into the cushions of the couch and lifted her arse. A single finger stroked between her cheeks and awoke nerves she'd never known existed.

She was completely dry back there, but the soft pad of his digit explored uncharted territory. As he pressed against her puckered hole something snapped open inside her and she felt her climax explode.

"Oh. Oh."

She couldn't think, couldn't comprehend anything except the overwhelming pleasure. The world detonated and she came hard. Her body clenched down around his penetration. Peter continued to drink her down, eagerly consuming her orgasm.

Tremors racked through her and she fell back into the couch, shaking. The intriguing pressure against her arse disappeared, but he continued to stroke his fingers slowly inside her pussy.

"Now that was unexpected," she panted, shocked and curious.

Peter lifted his head, his gaze smug and satisfied. Jane cupped his jaw and drew him up. She kissed him, tasting her own muskiness on his lips.

"Next time?" she asked.

He nodded. "Unless I'm too impatient to wait for a proper setting," he agreed. "Soon. We have plenty of time. I'm not in a rush."

"I'm not going anywhere either," she said.

Jane knew neither of them was speaking literally. Her search had clearly unearthed something and likely they'd need to act on it, whether that meant returning to headquarters or something else. In a vague way, they were each stating their commitment to the romance, or relationship blossoming between them. The fact they were both willing to see where it led unknotted a small tension she hadn't realized sat in her stomach.

She had no idea what the future held, but knowing Peter was as intrigued as she was helped give her confidence. They were in this together.

"I'll need five minutes to clean up again before I check what we've got," she said. "Do you want to wash up first?"

Peter stood and headed to the bathroom. Jane got to her feet and put her clothes to rights. She'd need a lightning quick shower. Her thighs and arse were slick with her cream and Peter's saliva. Her clothes were also far more rumpled than usual. A quick change wouldn't hurt her at all.

When Peter returned she gave him a quick kiss as she passed him. Jane gathered a new outfit then she went into the bathroom for the fastest freshening up ever. They might finally have a lead and she didn't want to waste too much time. Deeply curious, she wondered if they might finally crack the case.

Chapter Six

Peter didn't think he'd ever known a woman to shower and change as quickly as Jane just had. It wouldn't have been seven minutes from the second she stepped foot into the room to coming out again. He'd been debating with himself whether to sneak a look on her laptop when he heard the shower faucets turn off. Glancing at the clock, he'd noted she'd been in there less than five minutes.

ForestQueen was full of constant surprises.

He grinned to himself. Jane blew his mind, not just with her sexy body and delicious responsiveness, but her sweetness, her intelligence. She was curious and tenacious. If it wasn't for the fact she seemed happier at headquarters and not out in the field, he might have tried to convince her to get rated and be his new partner.

The dangers he frequently faced though, and the knowledge he wanted her in his life and bed as a romantic partner, not just a work one, had him holding back. He needed to take this slowly. Their leap from friends into more had been unexpected but inevitable. He didn't want to scare her off, or move too quickly and lose her.

Peter was discovering his happiness was far more tightly wound up in her than he'd previously acknowledged. She was fast becoming a necessity for his life, not just a passing fancy.

"Okay, let's see what we have," Jane said as she hurried into the room. Her hair was still tied up in a messy knot on top of her head, presumably to keep it dry while she showered. Her skin was dewy fresh, her cheeks and lips pink either from the hot water or possibly their dalliance earlier.

Those dark, fathomless eyes were pools he could happily drown in forever. Sadly, right now they were focused on work and not filled with sexual heat and longing as they had been.

Jane's mind was clearly back, concentrating on the code. Peter was amused, surprised at his own easily shifted priorities. He watched Jane, amazed anew at her talent. She moved her fingers so fast over the keyboard—with barely a glance to check her position, too—that it appeared like she flew. She nearly blurred as all ten digits were utilized.

He'd hate to be in a speed-typing contest against her.

"Hmm," Jane frowned.

Peter glanced over her shoulder, but she tabbed from one window to the next so quickly he couldn't make sense of any of it. He remained quiet, letting her think or just focus on whatever it was she was doing so well.

"Well we might have something," she said slowly. "Or it could be one of those coincidences I warned you about earlier."

"Let's have it, we can decide together if it's useful or not," Peter replied.

"Well, most of the archived files the hacker seemed interested in were based around the Middle East," she said. "I know the war in Afghanistan and before that Iran and Iraq means Britain has had interests for twenty years or more in those countries, but doesn't it seem strange to you that rather than the seeming random selection of cases and files, the hacker seemed to be searching missions related to that area?"

"It could, or it could be a coincidence," Peter admitted. "As you said, there must have been hundreds, maybe thousands of various cases and agents sent over there in the last twenty or thirty years."

"But if the hacker was doing this at random, there'd be other files too," Jane pointed out reasonably. "Russia, China, Japan. There are plenty of other countries we've done work in. I bet if you did a search over the last ten years, we'd have had some connection or interest in every country in the whole world. So to have all these cases be related some way to the Middle East... I don't know. It does seem like a link to me."

"Okay, let's run with that," Peter agreed. He was nervous it might be a deliberate red herring to mislead them, but they had to start somewhere. "What kinds of files were tampered with?"

"Well none were changed that I could see," Jane said as she scrolled down the screen. "But a lot were connected with informants in Qatar."

"Really? Qatar?" Peter mused. "They've become quite the power base in the Middle East in recent years."

"They've got plenty of oil and natural gas rights," Jane agreed. "And have made a name for themselves acting as the middleman in many agreements between more typically hostile countries, like Iran and Afghanistan, and the rest of the world."

"I know a man who was based for a number of years in Qatar," Peter said slowly, the seed of an idea forming. "Tommy Brown had his finger on the pulse out there for quite some time."

"Can you get in touch with him?" Jane asked.

"He's been back in London for, must be nearly two years now," Peter nodded. "I'd be surprised if he's lost touch with his contacts, but he hasn't been actively in the field for a while. It's a young man's game and Tommy came home to spend time with his family when he started getting close to fifty."

"Let me just try..." Jane typed furiously, then exclaimed in delight.

Peter looked over her shoulder and saw the log in page for their secure network. "Remote access is back up?" he was surprised how fast that had happened.

"Only certain features," Jane replied. "We can't be offline for too long or field agents would start to panic. Protocols have to be maintained, miss too many check-ins and there'd be serious consequences. I'm guessing the archives will be locked down for a while, since that's where the hacker was looking, but people's private drives and emails should be up and running. Yes."

Peter watched as Jane accessed her email account. "Let me see if I can pull up active agents," she continued. "Here we go. Thomas Brown. I've got his current details, can you write this down?"

Scrambling for pen and paper, Peter then noted the phone number and address Jane read out. Peter could sense the case moving along, but it was unusual for him to still feel so largely in the dark. They had an unknown attacker looking for information he still didn't have a clue about. Peter was used to the shadows, but after a while he always had a good understanding for any given situation.

This time he felt lost. It was possibly the new factor of Jane putting him off his game. The chemistry and attraction he felt for the beautiful lady was undeniable and a constant distraction, but if he was honest it wasn't that. He felt out of his depth with all the technology. So much of this case was beyond his ken.

Peter was used to being in control, or at least understanding all the facts surrounding him. This time, he could only comprehend what Jane explained to him. And secondhand information — no matter how reliable the source and trustworthy the case — was unheard of for him.

He didn't know the correct questions to ask, or buttons to push. Hopefully something Tommy knew might help lead him and Jane in the right direction.

He got his mobile from his pocket and glanced at Jane.

"What do you think?" he asked her. "Should we meet up with him, pick his brain for anything unusual that's been happening in Qatar or the Middle East? We need something to indicate to Tommy what it is we're looking for."

Jane seemed to understand what he was getting at. She bit down thoughtfully on her lower lip, a sensual act that captured his attention.

"The hacker had to be looking for information," she summarized. "We should look back as far as twenty years ago."

"Only twenty?" he asked, knowing their records stretched back further than that.

"Anything older than twenty years is maintained off site in a different location," Jane explained. "And a large portion of the records more than thirty years old are in paper format anyway. We can always go further back, but I think a good place to start is five to twenty years."

Peter nodded. That sounded sensible to him. He still felt nervous, a lot of the case seemed to him like trying to capture the fog on an early morning. It was worse than his usual floundering around, grasping at straws. They were at least solid. This whole situation felt very uncertain to him.

But one thing his years in this field had taught him was that the more questions he asked, the more rocks he upended and the more information he got. And the more pieces of the puzzle helped you see what was really going on.

So asking random questions it was.

Peter dialed Tommy's number.

"Brown," Thomas answered.

"Tommy, Peter Abrams here. How's it going, mate?"

"Yeah, good. You?"

"Going well. Look, my partner and I need to pick your brain about something," Peter raised his eyebrows at Jane suggestively. "We're looking into a case and think it might hark back to a mission connected with the Agency and the Middle East. Or Qatar in particular. Can we meet up? Chat?"

"Sure," Tommy sounded interested but puzzled. "But you realize I haven't been active over there for a few years. The missus and the little ones have kept me here and I'm out of touch with some of the more recent changes. John Brennan might be a better bet, though getting a hold of him might prove tricky if you're in a hurry."

"This stuff is linked to the past," Peter added. "We're thinking of starting five to twenty years in the past. Maybe further, but we're not sure yet."

"Oh, well in that case, sure. Where do you want to meet?"

Peter thought for a moment. "It's almost happy hour. Do you remember the pub we used to play darts in, when you were on leave?"

"Is that joint still open? Sure. Give me an hour and the first round is on you."

Peter hung up the phone. He noticed Jane was saving everything from the hard drive onto the laptop.

"I'm still a bit nervous about how the hacker got into the system without seeming to raise any red flags," she said without turning around and look at him. "The time it took to do everything should have set off alarms."

"Like when you enter a house, the security system gives you five or ten seconds grace to enter the password before it sets itself off," Peter guessed.

Jane nodded. "Exactly. There's a lag period, for people who've been incorrectly redirected, or mistyped their URL. That sort of thing, though it's really rare. But even with all the correct passwords and knowledge, there's just no way I can see someone could hack in without setting off the alarms. It's driving me mental not knowing how they gained access."

"Okay," Peter was following her now. "But what are you thinking? How can you find out how the hacker got in?"

"I've got a few ideas," Jane hedged. "I'm not sure any of it will work, but if we're going on the move I want all the data on my laptop. I can keep it powered up in my backpack and running searches remotely while we travel. I'll turn the sound of the chime up, so if it finds anything I can step aside and check it out."

"Knowing how the hacker gained entrance will tell us something about them?" Peter suggested.

Jane shrugged. "Not necessarily. The important thing is it will show us wherever the leak is and I can let Bones know. We can fix it immediately. It's too late to stop the hacker gaining entrance now, but it'd be lazy for us to not block that route since we know there's one there. We might learn something, but I think it's more important to fortify our seals before the hacker returns, or worse, lets other hackers know about our breaches and we get flooded with other attempts."

"If the hacker had inside help we need to question the agent who helped them too," Peter pointed out with a grimace. "I don't relish the thought of outing a traitor, but we can't be blind to it either."

"I'm becoming less inclined to believe they had inside help," Jane sighed. "The database says no one has logged in from an unusual ISP. If someone from the inside had shared their log in details then a unique, or spoofed ISP would have been recorded on the system."

"Could our logging system have been corrupted? Or also hacked and altered?" Peter asked.

"It's certainly possible, though a lot of trouble." Jane frowned as she typed. "Bones will probably get a few analysts to check the system manually, to make sure it's clean. But I just don't think it will pan out, it doesn't feel right to me."

"Well hopefully Tommy will be able to give us a lead, or at least point us in the right direction."

They fell silent for a minute while Jane finished. She closed the laptop, the small lights still shone and showed the computer was running searches.

"We need to stop by a pharmacy," Peter said with a small smile.

Jane looked curiously at him, but he saw understanding dawn in those beautiful brown eyes. A light touch of color flushed on her cheeks and she simply nodded.

"Let me grab a bag," she said. "Then we can get moving."

Chapter Seven

"The Leaky Wheelbarrow?" Jane chuckled as Peter led them into a dimly lit pub.

"It's a classic," Peter reassured her.

Unconvinced, but amused, Jane kept silent as they slid into a booth. She looked around. It was a fairly standard pub. The walls held framed prints and large, flat-screen TVs showing various football matches being replayed. There was a lingering smell of old leather and underneath, the faint whiff of cleaner and beer. Half the stools around the bar were taken by a mixture of men in suits, ties loosened, having a pint before heading home after a hard day, and men in working gear, blue-collar guys.

No one had even glanced up as she and Peter had entered. She started to relax. It wasn't out of the realms of possibility that the hacker was a businessman or construction worker. Jane didn't have that feel from the case so far. Their quarry needed to spend a lot of time on the computer, working through various coding stages and needed dedication to this project. She doubted he or she was here right now.

Jane surveyed the large room and felt her heart stop. Two small CCTV bubbles were at either ends of the room. She blinked, and felt a small crawling sense of paranoia return.

"Do you think the hacker could have traced us here?" she said in a low tone, leaning into the table so she couldn't be overheard.

Peter glanced around and looked puzzled.

"What do you mean?"

"Over there, a CCTV camera," Jane tilted her chin and indicated.

"This hacker can't be omniscient," Peter reassured her.

It was a struggle, but Jane made herself nod and tried to calm her racing thoughts.

The pub was on the outskirts of the city. Busy, but not crushed. Close enough to London that Jane bet people dropped in and out regularly. A good place to meet and remain unobserved.

Except for that damn security camera.

The thought gnawed at her.

"How trustworthy is this contact of yours?" she couldn't help but ask.

Peter smiled at her, seeming patient with her concerns.

"Exceedingly. I know how delicate this matter is, Jane," he insisted. "I'm not trying to pooh-pooh your nerves. There is a guy—or girl—out there and I agree with what you said back in the parking garage. Sooner or later they will stop lurking in the shadows and come out into the open. They'll probably also be dangerous. People who have repressed their actions, who've held onto their control as long as possible, usually totally snap and go crazy when they do let loose. But we can't be jumping at every shadow. We need to get this done and carry on."

Jane nodded, he was right.

Her heart hammered though. She couldn't put the worry away—not yet.

"Okay," she said. "Humor me, please. The hacker jumps out from behind some potted plant as we walk up to the bar to pay the bill. He's a ninja and starts to attack us. What do you do?"

Peter grinned and for a moment her heart stopped. For just a split second all thoughts of danger and a crazy, repressed computer geek living in some kind of conspiracy world disappeared. Ensnared, Jane almost lost herself in that sexy blue gaze and the cheeky grin. Peter, however, took her snap question seriously, although he appeared amused.

"To be honest it would depend on exactly how he attacks us. If I can just grab him and try to talk him down, that's usually the response I try for first. I'd talk, ask him what he's so upset about, offer to help him. You'd be amazed how often people want to be listened to. They want to feel like their concerns are being heard and acted upon. Violence rarely solves issues and I've found the vast majority of people understand this."

Jane stared thoughtfully at Peter and found herself nodding. She was sure his response wasn't a common one, or even a socially acceptable answer. But she had to admit the truth in it. And one thing she knew about Peter, he knew both how to listen and how to talk. He was a silver-tongued devil when he wanted to be. He could talk anyone into practically anything.

"Okay," she agreed. "Thank you for being honest. And I have to admit, if this could be wrapped up peacefully, without any incident that would be excellent. But say our hacker is some hyped-up freak. Or high on drugs. Or just so angry, so crazy after repressing his concern for decades, what if you can't talk him down? What if he's just determined to kill us both and cut us into little pieces. What then?"

"You don't feel safe with me," Peter said shortly. He sat back in his seat and locked his gaze with hers. "Is that what you're saying?"

Jane took a deep breath and answered carefully but honestly, "That's not what I said, nor is it what I meant as an undertone." She thought for a moment then continued, "I think there's too much about this situation we still don't understand. Far too many variables. For all we know, this is actually some big underground movement, like Anonymous, and we're getting caught up in some huge web of deception. This could be a single tendril of a large, unwieldy beast and I don't want to spend the rest of my life looking over my shoulder, scared of every security camera and needing sixteen layers of filtering between my every keystroke and the truth of what I want to do. Can you blame me for that?"

"No," Peter said far more gently now. He reached over and took her hand in his, resting them both on the top of the table. "No, I think that's a perfectly rational response to the level of danger we're facing. But I'm telling you, I can keep you safe. I promise. Yes the situation is dangerous, even volatile, but that doesn't mean we can't come through it."

He spoke with such strength, such inner conviction she believed him instantly, without all the finer details.

"With your computer skills and intelligence," he continued, "and me bumbling alongside you, we're going to be fine."

Peter squeezed her hand. She smiled, feeling her nerves calm down.

"You believe me, right?" he said. She nodded without any hesitation.

"Definitely. I guess I'm not used to this, that's all. The paranoia and stress is just getting to me. But you're right, we'll be fine. We can sort it out."

Peter chuckled and her worry was replaced by the urge to lean in and kiss him. To feel his warm arms wrap around her and hold her tight.

Knowledge that Peter had a small box of condoms in his pocket burned into Jane's mind. His vest and jacket hid the bulge in his trousers, but he'd had such a proud, naughty gleam in his eye when he came out of the pharmacy, Jane couldn't get the image out of her brain.

Fantasies of how they'd use those condoms had kept her mouth dry while they'd stood, cramped, on the tube. The closeness of his body and the fact he smelled of her handwash kept her mind distracted.

"Do you think—" Someone entered and Peter's attention was caught. He lifted a hand but didn't call out. A tall, bulky man came toward their booth. A wedding band circled his finger. His close-cropped black hair had a heavy sprinkle of salt in it. Although his suit was well tailored, Jane got the impression this was a fit man just starting to put on the kilos as he became less active and more deskbound.

"Peter, you devil, how the hell are you?"

"Tommy." Peter stood and the men shook hands warmly. "Thank you for coming and helping."

"No problems, I could do with a pint and a bit of time off daddy duty," Thomas said with a smile.

"This is Jane," Peter introduced her. "Jane works in the tech division. It's she who started this ball rolling."

"Lovely to meet you." Thomas nodded and Jane replied with a smile. She had to force herself to focus and not be so bloody paranoid. Peter was right, the hacker couldn't be everywhere at once, and she really did trust him to take care of her.

Besides, no one had telepathy. The hacker didn't have some magical crystal ball. She and Peter would be fine. Jane knew she had to forget about her anxiety and get on with the job.

Peter ordered them all a drink and when the waitress had left he turned to look at Thomas. "Tommy. Have you heard about what went down this afternoon?"

"Only the bare bones of it," Thomas returned in a low tone. "Is this connected?"

"The majority of the files the intruder was trying to investigate were connected with old cases in the Middle East," Jane added, wording herself vaguely on the off chance someone could hear them speak. "We're hoping you can shed some light on what might be motivating our uninvited friend."

Thomas glanced from Peter to Jane then back to Peter again. "You're kidding? What, you want me to summarize twenty-five or so years of work in fifty words or less? Peter, come on, mate. You know it doesn't work like that. Do you have anything more to help a bloke out?"

Peter glanced at her and Jane decided to take it that he was giving her a chance to start them off. Jane thought for a minute then spoke, "My knowledge about the Middle East and Qatar in particular is pretty shaky, just what you see on TV and read in the papers. What's the political climate like, say in the last decade or so?"

The waitress brought their drinks over, two pints of beer for the men and a gin and tonic for Jane. Jane sipped, Peter also had a small drink, but Tommy took a long pull from his glass before setting it on the table.

"Okay. Starting around the Persian war, Qatar seemed to make the beginnings of change," Tommy said. "They were a base for the coalition troops, the first olive branch and reason behind why the Agency, and others, could get a foothold in the Middle East. Liberalization was slow, but compared to the other countries—Iraq, Syria, Egypt and such—they're light years ahead of the pack."

Jane nodded as Tommy continued.

"When the US invaded Iraq, Qatar again acted as their launching base. They've been active in pursuing an Afghan peace deal, all through this latest war. They facilitate talks, exchanges and basically act as a go-between for the Western politicos and the Middle East."

"So they're a known middleman," Jane surmised. "Have either side been particularly upset by anything? Felt betrayed?"

Silently she began to worry. If the Agency had been hacked by terrorists she was well out of her depth. But what would they want with old files? And organizations like Al Qaeda didn't mess around hacking into archive databases. If they felt threatened by the Agency surely they'd have instructed one of the local cells to do something far more devastating?

It was a point she couldn't ignore, but Jane hoped she was just getting paranoid. The thought lingered though, and she decided regardless of what they found, she'd need to report to Bones sooner, not later.

"What stands out for you?" Peter asked as he took another sip of his drink. "Big things—particularly connected to the Agency. Stuff that would be reported on and archived once the case was closed or gone cold."

"I'm trying," Tommy insisted as he finished his drink. "But like I said, stuff happened almost every day. It's a different world out there—you know what I mean, Pete. Double-crossing, backstabbing and suspected turncoats. It's a hundred times worse out there in the desert. Paranoia is a way of life. Thinking some shadow around the corner is listening in out of sight. Or that the crackle you hear on your phone, or the shaky reception on your Internet is actually a tap, or multiple people listening in from all angles. It's a bloody nightmare. Particularly since Qatar is the supposed safe zone. You have people from all divisions, and not just ours, tripping over each other. Informants sell the same piece of information six times then melt into the background never to be heard from again. And you want me to give you the highlights from almost an entire career worth of two decades of this mess?"

"We just need a starting point," Jane tried to soothe Tommy. She could tell he genuinely wanted to help, but the situation was a lot more convoluted than she'd imagined. Much of her guilt for not being able to unravel what the hacker had sought eased. Clearly the politics and landscape in the Middle East was even messier than she'd previously understood.

"If you had to list the five biggest things, what would they be?" she asked. "Think along the lines of cases gone wrong. Tragedies connected to the Agency or a mission. Regrets. What leaps into your mind?"

"There was a case back at the turn of the century." Tommy said. "Must have been '02. It wasn't that long after 9/11, everyone was focused on the new War on

Terror but a lot of the structure hadn't been settled in as yet. There was a massive bombing. IUDs. We must have lost four or five agents. The Americans lost a few as well. I think there was an Aussie or two in the mix also. Bloody mess it was. We scrambled to retrieve the data they'd been collecting, but it was still quite new to us all. Trust wasn't high, even though there was no reason to doubt the Qatar nationals."

"It's always difficult when everyone's settling into a new structure," Peter agreed. "Relationships aren't built, trust is shaky and everyone's walking on eggshells feeling their way through. We'll need their names. What else?"

"A couple of female agents didn't last." Tommy drank and shook his head. "Bloody shame, that. I mentioned that liberalization had progressed and that wasn't a lie, but damn some of those men have backward notions. These women had been trained and weren't aggressive types. But they were modern. It got too much, being constantly overlooked and brushed aside. Not by our lot, but ignored by people they were supposed to be working with. And that doesn't include how hard it was for them to do something like walk down the street after hours and not be constantly approached by others. Like I said—a whole different world out there."

Jane made a note to look into all female agents who had been assigned to Qatar over the years. She couldn't imagine how difficult it must have been to work in an environment where so many of her supposed colleagues thought she was lesser just because of her gender. Or where she'd hesitate to walk outside because she'd be seen as fair game. She'd not thought about the fact it was a whole different society over there.

Could the hacker be an old agent? Someone who had retired? The thought intrigued her and for a moment Tommy and his musings faded into the background. It could certainly explain how they'd got into the system undetected, but why wouldn't they have the correct passwords to enter the archived system? An old agent could just call someone up, a friend, co-worker—hell, one of management or Bones—and get a temporary code. They could even request files be faxed over a secure line. Why hack in at all? While it was true retired agents couldn't review active files, or be briefed other than in generalities on what was current, they could certainly have access to closed cases.

Still, something about that sounded far more believable than many of the theories she'd been entertaining until now. It ticked a lot of the boxes she needed. Jane moved her glass to the side and pulled out her laptop. She realized Tommy had paused.

"I'm sorry, please excuse me," she apologized. "Keep going, I just want to check on something really quickly."

Jane connected to the system and searched for retired agents who had recently logged in. There was a wonderfully small number, completely manageable. Jane ran a cross-check between the names and their personnel files.

"...but the informant was never on the records officially?" Peter said.

Jane tuned back in as the laptop searched.

"No. A lot of these blokes didn't want it on any records who they were or where they lived," Tommy agreed. "And no one out here minded. Things were still quite unstable back then."

"Okay, anything else?" Peter asked.

Tommy drank while he thought and shook his head. "I think that's it, mate. Certainly for everything that immediately comes to mind. I can keep thinking and give you a call if anything else crops up."

Jane opened her mouth, about to ask for the details of the events he'd already mentioned, but her laptop beeped. A few keystrokes and she had the files all sorted.

"Hmm," she mumbled as she tabbed through the results. "These first three have been consulted recently on cases. Wait. Here. Warren Sandford died back in 2002 and somehow managed to change his password and email account recently. He was a courier and made a number of trips into the Middle East to collect data."

"I remember him," Tommy said immediately. "That was tragic. I actually flew back and attended his memorial. It was only weeks after that roadside bombing I mentioned. He came to collect the intelligence we'd scavenged from the blast. He'd made a number of trips into Qatar in the previous few months. After his death we found out that he'd been put onto some 'watch' list. We believed terrorists got their hands on the list and he was killed in a highly suspicious car crash on the way to the airport when he was returning home. Tragic."

"It says here he had a wife," Jane said scrolling through his record.

Tommy nodded. "Yes, I met her at the memorial. Umm... Anne?"

"Alice," Jane corrected, flying her fingers over the keyboard as she checked online records. She looked at Peter. "She still lives in London. Her address is still current."

Peter drained the last of his pint. Jane took paper and a pen from her backpack and jotted down the woman's name, age and address. She wished there was time to do a deeper background check on her, but Peter seemed ready to go now. Things moved fast in the field, Jane recalled. While she'd love to have all her ducks lined up, they didn't have that luxury. If the widow was the culprit she'd already had hours to scrub her computer clean. For all Jane knew, Alice might have already packed up her home and be in the process of leaving the country, or getting ready for another attack on their system.

Minutes later Jane had packed her bag again and shook Tommy's hand.

"Thank you so much," she said. "You've really helped us progress."

"Always happy to help," Tommy replied and chuckled as he held his hand out to Peter. "Let me know how it pans out."

They stood and left the pub. Tommy pointed toward the tube station. "I'll catch you both later, right?"

"Absolutely, mate," Peter clapped him on the shoulder. "Thanks again."

Tommy left and Peter hailed a taxi. Jane's brain whirled dizzyingly. "TruthSeeker," she said in a low tone.

Peter glanced at her and opened the door. "What?"

"TruthSeeker," she repeated. "That was the hacker's screen name. What if it's really Alice? Looking for answers into her husband's death?"

Peter's blue gaze narrowed thoughtfully, but he remained silent. Jane climbed into the taxi and sat down. Peter followed her in and slammed the door closed. Jane gave the driver the address and they set off into the busy evening traffic. Jane glanced at Peter.

"This will take a while, we're in the rush-hour crush. Will you have enough to cover it?" she asked.

Peter tapped the pocket in his vest. "Corporate card. We're fine."

Silence fell between them. Finally, Peter spoke again. "If you really think it's her maybe we should call it in."

Jane licked her lips and thought about it. She pulled out her laptop again and checked the database. "There's no record of her being...one of us," she replied, mindful that while the driver appeared to be paying no attention, she wanted to remain oblique. "No training, no details at all other than her husband," Jane finished. She closed the laptop again and returned it to her bag. "That doesn't mean she wasn't our party, but between us we should be able to keep a handle on the situation, don't you think?"

"Do you really think you can handle it?" Peter asked.

Jane leaned toward him and brushed a kiss on his cheek. "I'm a big girl. I can handle myself. Why don't we start gently. If she gives off a weird vibe we can retreat and call in the cavalry. How does that sound?"

"I hate the thought of you being in danger," Peter whispered.

Jane leaned into him and wrapped her arms around his shoulder, hugging him tightly. "I'm not saying I'll chase her down, wrestle her to the ground," Jane murmured into his ear, struggling not to laugh at the mental image. "But we're here, on our way and we have the first solid lead we've got all day. If we called Bones, or Preston, there'd be paperwork and meetings, briefings to update other agents and blah blah blah. All we're doing is going to see a widow to ask her a few questions about her husband. How dangerous can it be?"

"Famous last words," Peter said, his lips only an inch from hers.

They kissed and she relished the softness of his mouth. His hands were warm on her back, drawing them both close together. The car stopped and they broke apart. Jane looked and they were merely at a red light. She glanced at the driver and he was very studiously avoiding the rearview mirror.

She chuckled and patted the box in Peter's pocket.

"We'll have a chat and call it a night. It will be easy, just you wait and see," she promised.

Chapter Eight

Alice Sandford lived in a neat flat on a quiet street. There were framed English landscapes dotting the wall from the entrance into the living room. The couch and stuffed chairs had a number of well-worn cushions giving them life. The pretty scenes on the cushions looked personally cross-stitched. Although the house didn't appear that of a spinster—no profusion of vibrantly painted flower vases and lace doilies—it seemed equally clear to Jane that it'd been quite some time since the man of the house had been in residence.

The house was near silent, only the faint tick of a clock coming from another room. Jane and Peter sat on the couch, a respectable distance separating them. Jane felt faintly as if she were visiting an aunt for tea. Alice returned with a tray and set it on the table before pouring them each a cup and placing a small plate of biscuits next to the milk and sugar bowl.

"You're from the Agency, you said? Is this about Warren, after all this time?" Alice asked. She seemed mildly curious, but in a watered-down, flat kind of way. Something about Alice made Jane think of her as beaten down by life. As if she'd received as many kicks as she could manage, but she was still standing strong and determined to march onwards.

Jane had an awful time trying to picture her as some hacker, breaking laws and careless about the privacy act. It didn't gel with the middle-aged woman offering her the social niceties and seeming to have only a passing interest in their curiosity. There was no guilty pause, no spark of passion, no apparent knowledge or understanding of why they were making this call.

The hacker wouldn't expect to be traced, but they'd certainly know the Agency would be looking for them. If this was an act covering her guilt, it was a stellar one, worthy of awards. Jane had the sinking sensation they might have made a terrible miscalculation.

"What can you tell us of his passing?" Jane asked in a gentle tone.

Alice took her seat and sipped her tea. She shrugged. "Not a lot. He was a courier, low level, and he always insisted it wasn't risky. I should have known that wasn't quite truthful, for he never talked about any details. But he was serving his country, doing his duty, it was important to him. I was proud of him."

There was no heat, no anger or bitterness in her tone. This was clearly something she'd long ago come to terms with. Jane thought there might have been a faint hint of wistfulness behind Alice's words, but she doubted losing one's husband relatively young was ever going to be a wound that healed. It all seemed completely natural to her.

Jane felt a bit guilty for intruding.

"Did Warren ever work with a partner?" Jane asked, scrambling to try to find a reason for Sandford's email account to mysteriously become active recently. "Or a close friend who also worked in the Agency?"

Alice shook her head. "As a courier he never traveled with anyone—he effectively worked alone. He had a boss of course. A Mr. Mason, I believe. But Warren would spend most of his time either here at home, or traveling to pick up or deliver documents. It wasn't like what you see in the movies—there were no big car chases, no slinky cocktail parties, martinis and a different woman at each port. He was, for the most part, a regular businessman who simply traveled more than many. I'm sure he had friends. I could look up my address book from those days, maybe find a few names for you, but after the usual condolence period I lost touch with the few there might have been. People move on."

Jane was starting to feel like this might be a dead end. Had they really been so wrong?

"Is that Warren, your husband?" Peter chimed in for the first time.

Jane glanced to where he indicated. On the mantelpiece there was an old photo in a wooden frame. Clearly taken by an amateur, possibly Alice herself, it captured a bright, azure blue sky at an odd angle. A handsome man with scruffy stubble and mousy brown hair sat on top of an annoyed looking camel. A young girl with sun-bleached blonde hair clung to him, the biggest smile possible spread over her face.

"Yes," Alice said.

Jane couldn't help but notice the reticence in the woman's tone.

"That's Warren in Egypt, having a camel ride," Alice said in a repressive voice.

Peter gently pressed her. "And your daughter? A family holiday?"

"Warren loved the Middle East," Alice said reluctantly. "He found a lot of beauty in the arid desert. The tribal people, or many of them at least, are a beautiful group. Hospitable. Caring. Deeply spiritual. There are many radicals who taint their name, but much like anywhere in the world, most of those you meet are wonderful. We went on a short vacation, yes."

"How old is your daughter now?" Jane asked, trying to sound interested without becoming pointed.

"Nicole is seventeen. She was five when Warren passed, but she still has a number of vivid memories of him she's retained."

"Where is Nicole?" Jane pressed.

She could tell this was the exact moment Alice dug her feet in. Became stubborn. "What is this really all about?" Alice demanded.

Jane placed her cup and saucer on the table and softened her tone so it was placating. "Mrs. Sandford, we've been completely honest. We just have some questions about your husband's death and the circumstances that surrounded him at that time."

"Someone accessed his accounts recently and we're trying to determine who that might be," Peter added.

Alice looked puzzled but no less annoyed. "Warren's been dead for a dozen years," she pointed out. "And I strongly doubt I know more about his death than you do. No one from the Agency would answer our questions, or even communicate with us after the first few times. We were just shut down, ignored and brushed aside. Unimportant. We never even got his body to bury, let alone answers that you seem to seek after all these years."

Jane was surprised and struggled to hide it. When she thought about it though, it made a sad kind of sense. Anything about the situation was likely classified. The widow, and child, would be kept in the dark. Fed platitudes about how he died serving his country and given a sympathetic pat on the back.

It wasn't something she enjoyed admitting, but she certainly believed it. The Agency's intentions might have been good, but it would have been a bitter pill to swallow, had she been in Alice's situation.

"Have you or Nicole accessed your husband's old records?" Jane asked. The time for softness was passing, they needed answers and Alice's stubbornness indicated they might be on the right path after all. "Did he leave behind a diary—or a card with his passwords on it? Does Nicole have friends who are hackers?"

"Hackers?" Alice repeated.

Jane winced and knew immediately she'd stepped in it. Alice placed her cup and saucer down with a clatter and drew herself so her back was ramrod straight. Outrage vibrated from her.

"You bloody Agency people think you're so righteous," Alice vented. "Perfectly willing to break the rules for Queen and country but looking down upon anyone trying to get the same answers. Let me tell you something about the situation, young lady. You're searching for answers, you say. Well join the bloody club. Twelve years now we've been kept in the dark, ignored and discarded like a used tissue. I made phone calls. Wrote letters. Even tried to see your bloody managers—case leaders, I believe they're called—in person. Just to get a few little details or my husband's body. I got plenty of tea and sympathy. But not a single straight answer."

"Madam," Peter interjected. "The international privacy law and secrets act were almost certainly in play here. I'm sure the men you spoke with wanted to help you, but—"

"Oh pooh." Alice sniffed disdainfully. "You bloody lot hold up that stupid secrecy act like it's a writ from God himself. Do you think I didn't offer to sign nondisclosure forms? Do I look like a woman who wants to throw herself into a terrorist cell and do heaven knows what? I wanted some of these precious answers you seem to be seeking, for myself and my daughter. So we could have closure. That's it. No big conspiracy, no convoluted, devious plan full of backstabbing and dead drops. I wanted to be able to explain to my little girl what happened to her daddy. That's it. But no, no one could lift a finger and give me even crumbs from the table."

Jane felt horrible, but finally she at least felt like they were getting somewhere.

TruthSeeker.

"So Nicole decided to find some answers for herself?" Jane guessed.

Alice glared at her, hot enough that Jane had to force herself not to wither under the scorn. "My daughter has nothing to do with this," Alice insisted. Jane could hear the wobble in the woman's tone and knew they were on the right track.

"Madam, I'm sorry you've been through this," Jane said honestly. "I think it's a horrible situation and I don't begrudge you the anger you rightly feel. But if Nicole has been a party to the hacking of Agency files, she could be in a lot of trouble."

"And you think I'll lead her to your door?" Alice said, her disbelief clear. "I don't bloody think so."

"Right now we're your best bet," Peter added his weight to Jane's. "This won't just disappear. If we don't find Nicole, others from the Agency will. And we now understand the backstory—Nicole has reasons for her actions. We can take that into consideration."

"She'll be safe with us," Jane insisted.

Alice glared at them both then looked to the mantelpiece and the happy photo there. A tear ran slowly down her cheek. "The world hasn't been safe for either of us since that day one of your bloody people knocked on my door and explained my Warren would never be returning home again."

Silence fell and Jane waited, mentally willing Alice to help them. A few minutes ticked by and Alice finally sighed.

"Nicole has a small flat in the city," Alice said in a low tone. "She divides her time between here and there. She's more like you people than she'd ever admit. Her core, her values and morals are firm and strong, but she's quite willing to bend or break the rules 'for the greater good'. When it comes to her father though, I think she'd walk barefoot through hell and back to get answers. And I don't blame her a bit."

"We understand," Jane replied. "We need to make this right, but I have no desire to haul her over the coals if we can work something out. I mean that."

Alice gave them the address and Jane stood. As they were escorted out, Jane couldn't remember ever feeling worse. Battered. Emotionally bruised. As she and Peter stood on the footpath she looked at him.

"That was awful. Are we really doing the right thing here?" she asked.

"We need to put this to bed, like you said," Peter admitted. "But I have to admit I have no desire to bring a young girl to headquarters in cuffs because she wanted answers about her father's death in the field twelve years ago."

"I signed up to bring down hardened criminals, to keep our country safe," Jane added. "Not to beat up already grieving people and hide the truth from them."

"And what if Nicole started selling her skills," Peter pointed out. "What if she became anti-government, or a sympathizer with some radical group. There are small steps leading down the wrong path, who are we to draw the lines?"

Jane tilted her head, acknowledging the hit. It still didn't sit properly with her, but she could see where he was coming from. "Alice is almost certainly calling Nicole even as we speak," Jane said. "This might be moot. We might arrive to find an empty flat and nothing to help us."

"Where would she run?" Peter pointed out. "She's lived here her entire life. Her school, friends, family are all here. Besides, if she's truly full of righteous indignation she'll want to argue with it, prove her side of the story. I think she'll be sitting right there, ready and waiting to verbally do battle with us."

"I hope so," Jane sighed. They walked toward the train station. "I think we've got enough to call Preston, don't you?"

"Yes," Peter said sadly. "Let's update him and get a fresh opinion. I don't think we should go too hard on the kid."

"Neither do I," Jane agreed.

"Okay." Peter pulled out his phone and dialed.

Jane took his hand in hers and threaded their fingers together. The casual intimacy felt wonderful, but it also meant she could stay close and hopefully hear both sides of the conversation.

"Preston," Peter said. "Abrams here. How are things back there?"

"Finally starting to calm down," Preston's deep voice boomed on the other end. "How are you and Jane doing?"

"Really well, actually," Peter cast her that wicked grin. "We've found a solid lead and might even know who's responsible."

"That's excellent. Do you need backup?"

"No, it's complicated," Peter hedged. "In fact, the Agency might be somewhat culpable, at lease for motive."

"I'm not following," Preston said slowly.

"If what we think is correct," Peter replied, "the child of a former agent was looking for answers to her parent's death. After years of being stonewalled by us and possibly just to flip us the finger, who knows, the suspect decided to take it upon themselves to find answers to their questions."

"That would be complicated," Preston agreed. "And certainly not the sort of press we'd want released. Sympathy alone would smear our name and paint us as the enemy. What are you thinking?"

Peter looked at her and Jane pointed to the phone then herself. They stopped walking and Peter leaned over. He angled the phone and bent so they both could hear Preston and speak to him.

"Sir," Jane said, "I think Peter and I will need to reserve judgment until we actually speak to the woman in question. "We spoke to the mother, the widow of the past agent. I honestly believe she's a good person, not a traitor or conspirator. From and because of the background here, I'm willing to have faith the daughter might prove misguided, angry and rebellious. Not nefarious or a traitor."

"Peter?" Preston asked.

"I have to agree," Peter added. "It's possible the daughter has taken a wrong turn somewhere and we might be faced with a jaded delinquent, or someone who isn't as innocent as we'd like to believe. But at this point in time my gut says the girl was after closure on her father's case. For herself and her mother."

"What about the virus?" Preston asked after a long pause. "If this kid is so clean why plant something that could have corrupted our files? Caused us weeks of delay or even seriously damaged our work."

"While that's true, sir, I think that was just a very convoluted warning system," Jane replied. "The virus was packaged up into different sections. Anyone with the level of skill the Agency hires should have realized, as I did, after a few of the packets were released that they were tagged to the files and been able to contain them. Which is what happened. Now I admit we might have just got lucky, but if this hacker had wanted to cripple us, she's certainly shown enough talent so far to have been able to do it overtly. She didn't need to lay out such an intricate web. She could have just hit us with the virus without any warning through the back channel she found and shot us down. Nicole has the talent from that, if this is the person we're seeking."

"Sounds like you're both won over," Preston sighed.

Jane couldn't really tell without seeing Preston's face, but she didn't think he sounded very happy.

"I believe we've discovered where the breach in the system is," Jane added. "A deceased agent's email account was effectively rebooted. New password and forwarding email logged."

"How is that even possible?" Preston asked.

"I can't prove it yet sir," Jane began hesitantly. "But I believe what I'll find when I look into it is that because Warren Sandford's account has lain dormant for so long, when Nicole tried to log into it she was asked automatically to change the password. Whenever the system is upgraded, one of the security measures built into the software is that all users are required to update their passwords the next time they log on."

"Okay, I'm following," Preston said.

"Being prompted to change the password," Jane continued, "Nicole could have had it reset to a random one by claiming she'd forgotten the previous one. This account hasn't been touched for over ten years. She simply inserted a new secondary email address, had the new random password sent to that one and changed the password to something for herself. It'd be easy to log in after that."

"So she could have been accessing our system for months, or years?" Preston sounded outraged.

Jane hastened to reassure him. "Actually the reason we found this thread to follow was because Warren Sandford was an idle account that had only been revived in the last few weeks. As I said I—well we—might be misreading the situation. We still have a number of questions for Nicole Sandford. But from what we've pieced together so far, I think there's a complex, emotional background to it. This isn't just some hacker proving themselves, or an attempt to infiltrate our files and perform treason. It's trickier than that."

"I trust your judgment," Preston finally said after a short silence. "I still think you'll need to bring her in, for debriefing and to write your reports if nothing else. I might want to speak with her myself, form my own opinions, and I have a feeling Bones especially will want to pick her brain and discover exactly how she found this loophole in our security. That will need to be fixed immediately."

"Understood, sir," Peter said.

"For now, I'll update Bones," Preston said. "And get him at least looking into this interesting twist about inactive email accounts. Might as well get a jump on that."

"Thank you, sir," Jane added.

"I expect to hear from you both once you've spoken to this girl," Preston insisted. "Keep me in the loop."

They both agreed and hung up.

"Do we really keep email accounts open for such a long time?" Peter asked as he put his phone away. "Sandford was killed twelve years ago."

"I didn't know they were left idle that long," Jane admitted. "But maybe until now no one's felt there was a problem with it. I knew they were kept active for a while after agents passed or retired. Informants often still give details of interest, or old procedures are kept in play just in case. It makes sense to keep those avenues open, especially if no harm can come from it."

"I've got contacts I haven't spoken to in years," Peter mused. "If one of them suddenly tried to get in touch I'd want them to be able to contact me. Okay, I can see that, I guess. Remarkable that she found it though."

"It will be interesting to hear what she has to say," Jane agreed.

Chapter Nine

Nicole Sandford was a tall, thin wisp of a girl with a shaggy head of blonde-brown hair. She took one glance from Jane to Peter after opening the door and pouted.

"Mum called," she sighed. "Warned me. I know legally I might be in hot water, but dammit, I have a right to know what happened to my dad. You can all go to hell if you don't believe me."

Jane felt a part of her heart break for the young lady, but tried to not let it show. "Can we come in?" she asked.

Nicole seemed to think about it for a few seconds. With a defiant look on her face, she shrugged with what Jane felt certain was feigned nonchalance. "Sure." Nicole stepped back. "Knock yourselves out."

Jane entered the flat and studied it. Nicole shut the door behind them then led them into the living room. Jane thought it was a typical flat of a broke student. The couch sagged and was at least second hand, if not more. It seemed like a relic scavenged from the 1970s.

Books were lined in neat stacks, a mixture of text books and dog-eared fiction paperbacks.

The only electric items visible were a brand new laptop and a router. Jane wasn't surprised the only area Nicole seemingly spent her money was on her trade. There were no mementoes or personal effects around. Jane wondered if there might be a few in her bedroom, or if she kept her private life at home with her mum.

Not offering them a seat, Nicole crossed her arms over her stomach and glared at them.

"If you've spoken with your mother then you know why we're here," Peter said in a gentle tone.

"How are you going to play this?" Nicole asked bluntly, not the least intimidated.

Jane admired her spunk.

"Are you the good cop and the lady is going to growl at me when I don't give you what you want?" Nicole continued. "I know how the world's changed. You can threaten to lock me up and not even charge me. Probably drop me in some hole somewhere and let me think about my actions like a naughty girl in time out. I'm not stupid, you know. I understand how this works."

"You've been here before?" Jane asked, surprised. Although clearly angry, she'd have bet Nicole was mostly bluster and outrage. There wasn't the cool, jaded air about her. Although an adult in all but the legal sense, Nicole still seemed like an angry girl seeking answers, not a master criminal bent on destruction.

"No," Nicole admitted, this time with less heat. "No, but that doesn't mean I don't know how to read or follow the papers. You'd have to be blind to miss how the rules changed after the attacks."

"So you admit you attacked the Agency?" Jane led her carefully.

Nicole cast her a scathing glance. "I didn't attack anything," she insisted. "I might have found a back door, cracked open. Hypothetically speaking I might have wedged a gap to slip though. But I am not a terrorist. I didn't attack you. Indeed, the Agency is responsible for my actions, if you get right down to it."

"Explain," Peter said. "I'm not really much of a tech, though I understand the basics of what you did. How is the Agency responsible?"

Nicole nodded, as if she'd worked something out. "She's the tech, you're the field agent? Protecting her? Fine, Mr. Agent. I bet you're a curious sort, a bloke who likes his answers and all his ducks lined up neatly and all the Ts crossed. How would you feel if someone you loved was taken from you? Killed? Would you want answers? Justice? Closure? Would you bend a few rules, rage a bit when people slammed doors in your faces for years? Huh? Do you think you might be a bit ticked off if you couldn't get your precious answers from a few simple questions?"

"I can imagine how difficult this must have been for you," Peter agreed in a low tone. "Especially considering you were just a child, growing up with a bunch of concerns and no solutions."

"Bollocks to that," Nicole spat out. "I don't need your pity. Mum and I wrote letters, dozens of them. We called and did everything by the book. All we got was a bunch of fake sympathy and doors closed in our faces. What was I supposed to do? Pretend none of it happened? Move along happily and carry on? Screw that. And screw your precious Agency and its secrets."

"What will you do, when you get your answers?" Jane asked.

Again Nicole just shrugged. "Have closure, I hope."

"You were so prepared, so thorough, why did you leave before you had these answers you sought? TruthSeeker," Jane added.

"I thought you were half decent," Nicole sighed and sat. She waved a hand half-heartedly and both Jane and Peter took seats on the lumpy couch. "If you managed to get that then you're as smart as I worried. Actually I wasn't as organized as you think. I'd been looking for a way in for months. When I stumbled upon the glitch that automatically let me reset the email address and password, I thought I'd hit the lottery. The need to find out about Daddy was like a fire in my head. There was no way on earth I could let it go."

Nicole sighed and glanced between them. Having started, it seemed to Jane like the story just poured out of her. "I only wanted to nose around," Nicole continued. "To get a scope of the land, so to speak. But once I'd logged in I realized there'd be ways of monitoring the activity in a dead man's account. I got paranoid. Figured it would only be a matter of time before it got shut down and I'd be locked out once again. I'd come too far, you see? I couldn't live with the thought I might waste the opportunity because I wasn't bold enough to seize it."

"And the virus?" Peter asked.

Nicole waved a hand dismissively. "I've been accepted to study Robotics at a local university, but most of my mates are coders of various forms. The Trojan was a final year project of a friend. It was something I had handy on my computer. When I realized I was effectively on a time limit it only took me a few minutes to break the virus into a few packets and rig them as cherry bombs to give me a warning if someone cottoned on to what I was doing."

Nicole turned to look with interest now at Jane.

"You're the tech. Was that you hot on my arse?" Nicole asked.

Jane grinned. "Sure was, you gave me quite a run for my money, especially if it was all on the fly like you say."

"Things just sometimes come together, you know?" Nicole continued. "I hadn't set out that minute to search the files. I wanted to nose around, sure, but it kinda snowballed on me. I needed to know how my daddy died. Why? I couldn't let it go. Wouldn't. Once I split the virus up and you set the first flag off, it was a cascade. I started ripping into the archive files, searching for my dad's. But you put it all together too quickly. I was hoping if I waited till some unearthly hour this morning I might be able to take a second bite of the cherry. Go in with a cooler head. Guess that's bollocksed up now, isn't it?"

"Let's not be too hasty," Peter said in a calm way. "I'm thinking we might need to do this by the book, smooth over some ruffled feathers and be smart about it."

"Smart? How?" Nicole narrowed her eyes, clearly suspicious.

"You're young, innovative," Peter pointed out. "Clearly intelligent and if you've been accepted into Robotics, you're one of the smartest in your year. We can use brains like yours."

"I am not going to work for the Agency," Nicole stated flatly. "I'm not going to lie to my mother, cause her more grief than she's already suffered. Secrets have already ruined our lives. I'm not going to add onto that. No way."

"We do business with consultants," Jane added. "You'd be an independent contractor. You could go to university. Even get a full-time job or start your own company. The Agency would merely tap you when we could do with some help, or we felt you could contribute to a case. Within reason you'd have your freedom."

"I'm sure there'd be terms and conditions," Nicole insisted. "Nondisclosure forms, privacy acts to memorize and all sorts of paperwork hoops to leap through."

"There would be some of that, yes," Jane replied, "but there'd also be benefits. Part of the initial agreement would be access to your father's files. Answers. And there's always the knowledge you'd be helping your country. Giving back. Doing the right thing."

Nicole didn't answer immediately. Jane could tell they'd landed a hook and the young woman was seriously considering her options.

"You two look like mid-level talent," Nicole finally said. "You're not suits. Management. Do you have the authority to offer that?"

"We're not the ones who will sign off on it, no," Peter said. "But we're certainly your first step into getting access to what you want."

"If I consult I'll get to pick and choose what I do, right?" Nicole asked.

"Within reason," Jane replied. "And to be honest, you mightn't always know the entire picture. That's a fact of life in espionage. For safety—ours and yours—cases are often multi-layered. You'll certainly know what's expected of you and what your goal is, but there might be other things that are kept above your understanding. You're a mature young woman, you should accept that."

"I'm not going to keep secrets from my mother," Nicole insisted. "That's nonnegotiable."

"Certain aspects of your work will be kept quiet," Peter replied. "But you should certainly have enough leeway to be honest with your mum without giving her some of the finer details."

Nicole licked her lips and nodded. "I'll give it some serious thought."

Jane stood then dug her purse out of her backpack. Jane handed Nicole one of her cards. "Sleep on it and give me a call tomorrow. We'll talk to our managers and see if a middle road can be negotiated. I'm sure we can find a place where everyone is satisfied."

"Access to my father's records is also nonnegotiable," Nicole demanded as she took Jane's card.

"We'd expect no less." Peter smiled. "You're a determined young woman, and an intelligent one. I hope we can work together sometime in the future."

Nicole pressed her lips together, neither agreeing nor arguing with the statement. Peter and Jane took their leave. Nicole closed the door quietly behind them. Jane glanced at Peter, feeling hopeful. They walked down the footpath together in silence.

"Well, what do you think?" Jane asked as they headed down the street.

"I believe we gave her hope and a few things to think over," Peter replied.

Jane glanced behind them as evening drew on, noting that Nicole had closed the curtains and a light shone behind them. "I agree. Do you think she'll call tomorrow morning? Should we have given her the option? Or made it more of a demand?"

"I'm not going to pretend to be an expert in teenagers or young women," Peter started. "But I certainly think giving her the illusion of choice and freedom was smarter than insisting. We offered her something she wants quite strongly, which puts us in a good position, at least for negotiations."

"I really don't want to screw her over," Jane sighed. "Or force her hand. But I'm not sure Bones — or Preston for that matter — will let her turn around and walk away, either. We've got some leeway, but not free rein."

Peter wrapped an arm around her shoulder. Jane leaned into him as they walked together. She felt comforted and glad he was there with her. Jane realized with a pang of sadness their case was practically wrapped up. There were still a few loose ends and she had no doubt a mountain of paperwork, and meetings awaited them in the near future, but it was undeniable they were pretty much done.

"We're much closer to my place," Peter said after a minute. "How about you come over for dinner. I cook a decent bowl of pasta."

"Dinner?" Jane teased.

Peter laughed. "I was hoping to be too smooth to outright state that you spend the night."

"Oblique references certainly have their place," Jane admitted. "But I wanted to be sure I wasn't accepting under false pretenses."

Peter stopped. Jane lifted her hands and ran them through his hair, mussing it so the curls sprang out.

"I'll need to brush those back again," he murmured.

"Don't, I love them," she replied.

Peter bent his head. She stepped up on her toes and met his lips with hers. They kissed slowly, without the heat and burning need their first encounter had. Passion still simmered — Jane could feel the electric connection between them. But she knew they had all night, and many more ahead of them. The urgency had throttled back, for now.

He drew her flush against his body. Jane thrust her knee between his thighs and felt the hardness of his cock press against his trousers. She lowered her hands to his back and held him tightly. The sharp edge of the box of condoms in his vest pocket pressed into her side.

Slowly he pulled away. Jane hummed low in her throat, sad at the loss but knowing they couldn't finish anything they started out here on the street.

"I'll get a taxi," he murmured.

"Good idea," she whispered. Jane kissed him chastely then let him go.

Peter looked up and down the street and raised his hand, summoning a cab.

Chapter Ten

Jane stepped into Peter's house and was pleasantly surprised. She'd expected a typical bachelor pad, all leather armchairs, dusty shelves, an empty fridge and dishes in the sink. The entryway was certainly Spartan, but clean and well-ordered. Peter locked the door behind them and Jane dropped her bag next to the coatrack.

She turned, a compliment on the tip of her tongue, but Peter pressed her into the wall before she could utter a word. Fire exploded from his lips as he kissed her hungrily. Almost immediately her need rose, matching his breath for breath. She fumbled with the buttons of his vest, eager to touch his flesh, to feel the heat of him beneath her palm.

Again, he took her unaware. Without lifting his mouth from hers, Peter bent and threaded an arm under her knees. He muffled her cry as he swept her into his embrace. The walls blurred as he carried her down the hall. He stepped into a room and although she wanted to look, he nipped his teeth at her tongue and her attention was focused completely on Peter.

Next thing she knew, Jane found herself lowered onto a soft bed. Peter followed her down and snapped on a lamp.

"Eager?" she panted.

"Ravenous," he agreed.

Clothes melted away as they each quickly assisted the other to strip. Peter managed to pull the box of condoms out of his pocket before Jane swept the vest and the rest of their clothes onto the floor. Taking advantage of his momentary distraction, Jane pushed Peter's shoulder, urging him to lie back on the mattress.

"You've tasted me," she said, "now it's my turn."

Taking her time, enjoying the power he gave her, Jane licked her tongue out over Peter's hard nipple. It beaded and she repeated the motion with his other. Trailing her fingers down his hard, muscled chest, she drank in each shiver and hiss when she found his sensitive places. The centerline of his chest proved especially rich.

She peppered kisses tenderly down his torso and couldn't help but notice how his cock stiffened impressively. His head became slick, his slit weeping clear fluid as she ran her hands over his hips and around to cup his arse.

"Are you ticklish?" she murmured, curious because Peter truly seemed very sensitive to her touch.

"No!" he insisted so quickly and with such vehemence she had to wonder if it was the truth.

"Really?" She raised an eyebrow at him. Just as she felt her power turn to arrogance, Peter turned the tables on her.

Tangling their legs together, he then twisted his hips and flipped her over. She crashed down into the bed.

Jane laughed. "Surely that's an illegal move," she insisted.

"All's fair, darling," he purred. "Besides, it's too early in our relationship for me to give such power over to you."

Jane stared at him when he mentioned their relationship. Her feelings ran far deeper than mere friendship, but everything had happened very quickly. Her questions must have been obvious, for Peter kissed her again slowly.

"You're not a passing fancy," he assured her when he pulled back. "It's a slow progress, but I'm falling in love with you."

"I'm on that path too," she replied.

Playful heat merged into a slow burn. Peter nudged her legs apart and willingly she spread them wide. Pressing her hips into the air, Jane lowered a hand to her pussy and caressed her clit.

"Condom," she reminded him.

Peter could hardly take his eyes off her touching herself as he groped for the box and slid protection on. He made a show of it, completely unashamed. Jane kept her labia parted with one hand and showed him exactly how she touched herself in the privacy of her own bedroom. Her fingers grew damp as her excitement heightened. When she returned pressure from her thumb to her clit, she fluttered her eyes closed and moaned at the sensation.

"Fuck but you're amazing," Peter breathed hard. "I want to learn all your secret spots and just how hard you like to be stroked. But today has seemed endless. I want to fuck you, right now."

"I'm waiting for you," Jane teased, though the fact she panted proved the truth in her words.

Peter lifted her hips higher. Jane reached out and helped angle his stiff cock correctly. Slick and needy as she was, he slid into her body slowly. He stretched her full. It took a moment for him to penetrate her fully. There was a faint burn as she adjusted to his girth, but it was a delicious, small pain.

While they were nestled together, Peter surprised her yet again. He paused and took her hand in his. Bringing her fingers to his lips, he then sucked each one, consuming her juices. The intimate act took her breath away. None of her previous lovers had ever so willingly tasted her.

Jane melted and fell another step further in love with this man.

She cupped his face and drew him down to her, kissing him passionately. A few curls fell over his forehead, the silky strands brushing her skin and heightening her arousal.

"Move in me," she whispered. "I want to feel you everywhere."

Softly, sweetly he obeyed. Jane's heart pounded in her chest and she lifted herself to meet his thrusts. At first the pace was excruciatingly slow. But as their breaths came faster, Peter's control slipped. She stared in his eyes, lost in the crystal blue gaze.

"You're magnificent," he panted and rolled onto his back, bringing her once more on top of him, astride his body.

Relishing the chance to again set the pace, she pushed them both harder. Up and down she drew herself, angling her body for the maximum friction. Peter cupped her breasts and squeezed her nipples. Sparks flew through her blood and Jane struggled to catch her breath.

She threw her head back, her curls fell down and heightened the pleasurable sensation. Faster and faster she pounded, wanting to wring every second, every moment dry.

It started in her stomach. A knot formed and grew hotter, harder. Then it blossomed and spread, running down to sing on her clit and up to the peaks of her breasts. Jane could feel the prickling sensation of her flush across her neck and chest.

"I'm close," she gasped.

Peter tweaked her nipples in response and surged higher inside her pussy. He was thick, hot and stiff. Jane glanced down at him and saw sweat beading his brow. He seemed to be beyond speech.

Grinning, proud of herself, Jane moved faster until the tension within her broke free. She screamed out her climax, shaking as she raced to culmination. Heat suffused her body as Peter rolled them back over and pressed his body heavily over hers. Jane lifted her legs and crossed her ankles around his waist.

Peter thrust once, then a second time deeply into her pussy and roared his own orgasm. They both lay spent, sweating and wrapped together. The air sounded with their shattered breathing. Minutes ticked by and slowly Jane became aware of the cool air on her skin.

Peter moved to the side, slipping from her. She kissed him tenderly on the lips then snuggled her head into his shoulder.

Finally she shifted on the bed. "You boasted about pasta, I believe?"

"Best spaghetti bolognaise you've ever tasted," he agreed without moving a muscle.

"I look forward to it." She nipped his ear lightly and sprang from the bed, feeling energized, as if she could conquer the world. "For now though, I'm going to log onto our game. I've got a few more moves up my sleeve. Now my honor as well as my reputation is on the line, I'm going to kick your arse on that chess board."

Peter laughed, then groaned.

* * * *

The following morning

"Maybe for a while we should take it case by case," Nicole said.

Jane was quite proud of the woman. She'd neatly braided her hair and wore a button down shirt and skinny jeans. Nicole had also called at nine a.m. on the dot, agreeing to meet and discuss matters. Jane had been in to work far earlier and had met with Bones. They'd discussed Nicole and the situation.

Bones had been gruff and initially unimpressed that Jane had suggested Nicole work for them, but her boss couldn't deny the skills they could learn from the young woman. Preston and Peter were supposed to be here any minute now to assist in the debrief.

A knock sounded on the door and Jane turned, expecting the two men. Instead, Bones appeared, carrying an old archive box through the doorway.

"I believe Ms. Harvey has a ton of nondisclosure forms for you," Bones said without introducing himself. "And believe me, young lady, there will be more meetings in your future regardless of what course of action you decide to take."

Nicole waited silently, her eyes glued to the box. Jane's heart went out to her, well able to imagine what it represented to Nicole.

"That said," Bones said a little roughly, "mistakes are possible. This is a good agency, one of the best. But we're human. And fallible. I can own to it, as do others you haven't met yet. You've given us quite a bit of trouble young lady, but everyone is allowed a few bumps in the beginning. Don't you think?"

At this Jane saw Nicole lift her gaze and stare at Bones. The elder man held her glance and the two studied each other.

"Yes," Nicole said in a strong tone. "Actions can be taken out of context. Misconstrued."

Bones nodded. He placed the box on the table in front of Nicole. "These papers don't leave the room. The data within them doesn't leave the four walls you're currently sitting within. A very small number of the documents have been removed, as they're too sensitive for your eyes, but everything you should need to know is here and more besides. I've decided this is a goodwill gesture on our part. This isn't a bribe, or confirmation of an offer of any sort. This is to right a past wrong, nothing further. Understood?"

Nicole nodded. "Yes."

"Well then," Bones hesitated. To Jane's astonishment he patted Nicole's shoulder then turned to leave. He stopped again in the doorway. "You may tell your mother what happened, but must keep the details vague and general. Should your mother wish to also sign the same forms as you, she'll also be welcome to a one-time viewing of this matter."

With that Bones left the room. Jane saw Peter and Preston hovering in the doorway. Nicole sniffed and removed the lid from the box. Jane could see the sparkle of tears in the girl's eyes. Standing, Jane left her folder behind on the table.

"I'll give you some time," she said. "Knock on the door if you need something. Someone will be outside."

"Thank you," Nicole said very softly, though she didn't lift her gaze from the papers.

Jane left the room and closed the door behind her. She took a deep breath, the atmosphere in the small room highly charged.

"Everything all right?" Peter asked as he touched her shoulder tenderly.

Jane nodded. "I think it will be once she reads those files. I've already explained to her the manner in which our lawyers will make her miserable if she spouts off, discussing anything. But you know what? I think she's going to be just fine. She's taking it seriously, and seemed interested in a few things I mentioned. "

"Do you really think she'd be willing to work with us?" Preston asked, looking skeptical.

"Not in a traditional way, no," Jane admitted. "But I think she's a highly curious, deeply intelligent woman who enjoys a good challenge. It wouldn't surprise me if certain cases that strike her interest get under her skin and she decides to work on the fringes."

"I remember a current field agent who started in a similar manner," Preston said with a grin and mock fierce look at Peter.

"Hey," he protested. "I might have been curious and enjoyed a good challenge, but I never broke in and tried to steal things."

"You're a terror when you're bored," Preston insisted, unconvinced.

"Well, I'm not sure that's going to happen too often anymore," Peter said.

Jane blushed, but grinned.

"I've got reports to file and a bunch of files to recover from the temporary drive where it was backed up yesterday." Preston coughed. With what might have been a cleverly hidden smile, he left.

Jane checked up and down the hall, then pecked Peter's cheek with a quick kiss.

"You talked Preston and Bones around," she said.

"Not true," Peter blushed. "It was your rallying for her that swayed them."

"Oh bollocks," Jane sniffed. "They were on the fence. You gave them both a nudge after I'd left."

"We can stand here and argue." Peter hugged her close. "Or steal a few seconds for far better purposes."

"You really are a knight in shining armor," she whispered in his ear.

"Maybe to you, my darling," Peter replied.

She chuckled and kissed him thoroughly.

About the Author

Elizabeth Lapthorne has been writing professionally since 2002. She has a number of books released and is continually surprised by how much fun she has starting a new book and discovering new characters and situations that they put themselves in. She enjoys going to the gym (usually to chew over her latest problem scene), is rarely without a partially read book and has a weakness for chocolate.

Elizabeth Lapthorne loves to hear from readers. You can find her contact information, website details and author profile page at http://www.totallybound.com.

Totally Bound Publishing

Home of Erotic Romance